THIS COOKBOOK BELONGS TO:

_____

_____

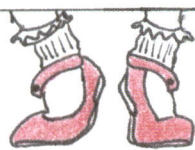

Ring Around the Rosie
A pocket full of posies
Ashes, ashes
We all fall down.

Ring Around the Rosie
A Collection of Children's Recipes
JUNIOR LEAGUE OF TYLER, TEXAS

Published by The Junior League of Tyler, Inc.

Illustrations © by Angelina Bruno Pearson

This cookbook is a collection of favorite recipes,
which are not necessarily original recipes.

Library of Congress Catalog Number: 2006923018
ISBN-10: 0-9607122-2-4
ISBN-13: 978-0-9607122-2-9

Edited, Designed, and Manufactured by
Favorite Recipes® Press
An imprint of

FRP

P. O. Box 305142
Nashville, Tennessee 37230
800-358-0560

Art Director: Steve Newman
Book Design: Starletta Polster
Project Editor: Cathy Ropp

Manufactured in China
First Printing: 2007
10,000 copies

Preface

After months of anticipation, The Junior League of Tyler, Inc., eagerly welcomes *Ring Around the Rosie* to its collection of cookbooks. *Cooking Through Rose-Colored Glasses* and *And Roses for the Table* have been popular for many years, and with the addition of *Ring Around the Rosie*, written for children with children in mind, everyone can enjoy the delicious recipes submitted by generations of Junior League of Tyler members and their families and friends.

A children's cookbook was the dream of Cookbook Chair Meredith Roberts, and over the last several months, through the efforts of the Cookbook Committee members and the active and sustaining members of the Junior League of Tyler, the dream has become a reality.

For those of us who like to cook and eat, *Ring Around the Rosie* is sure to provide fun in the kitchen for our children, grandchildren, young friends, or even just for ourselves. The recipes and crafts that are included in the book are for children to cook, eat, or create. Recipes in this book are a perfect way to share time with children, and at the same time, educate them about the kitchen, different foods, cooking, table setting, manners, and much more. Many thanks to all who submitted or tested recipes in preparation for publishing.

The Junior League of Tyler proudly presents this newest "rose" to its membership, the citizens of Tyler, and all who enjoy cooking, eating, or collecting cookbooks. Proceeds from the sale of our cookbooks have been used, and will continue to be used, to fund the numerous projects of the Junior League of Tyler, Inc. We hope you will enjoy this cookbook as much as the previous two and that you will share all three with your family and friends.

Mary Ann Cozby
President 2004–2005
Junior League of Tyler, Inc.

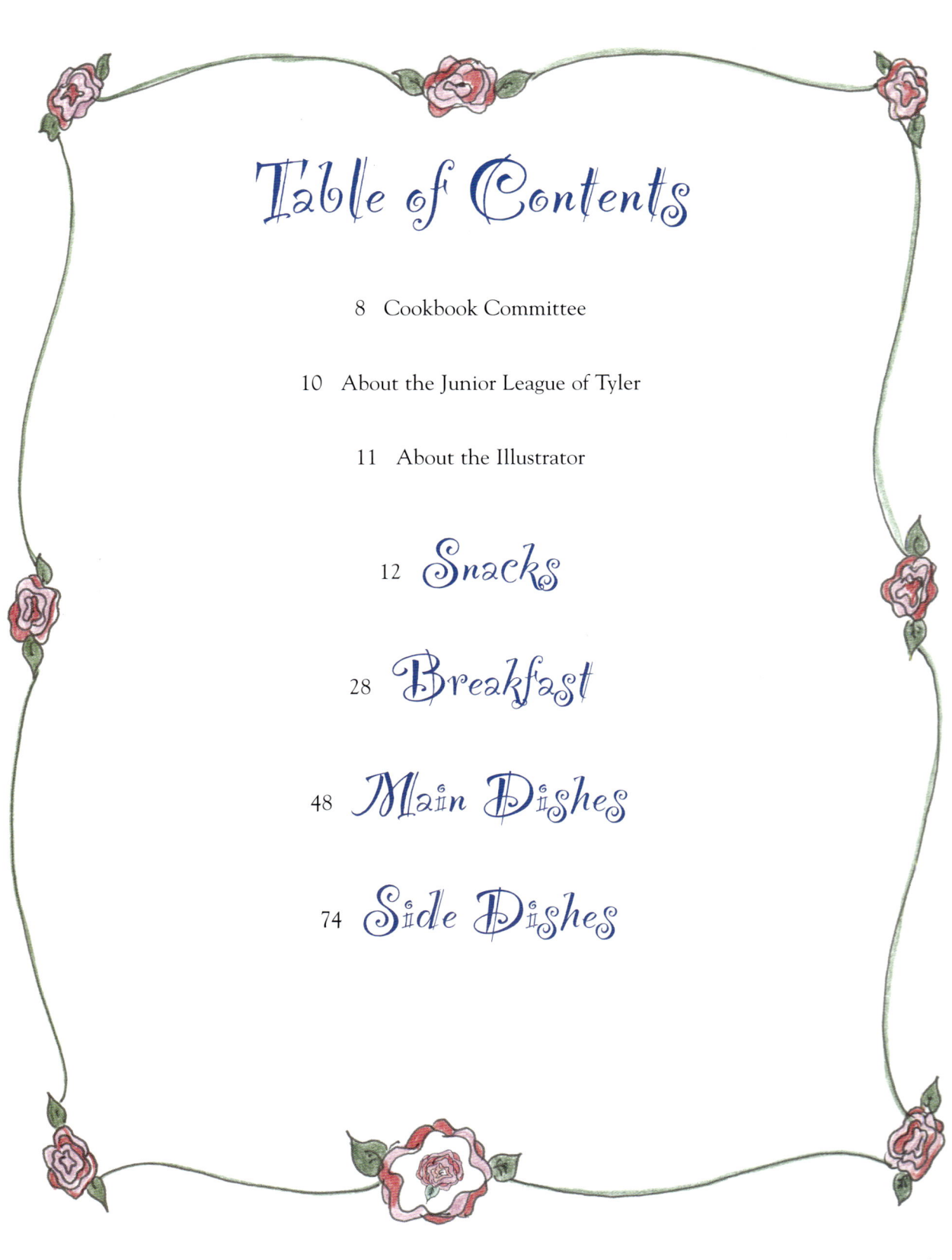

Table of Contents

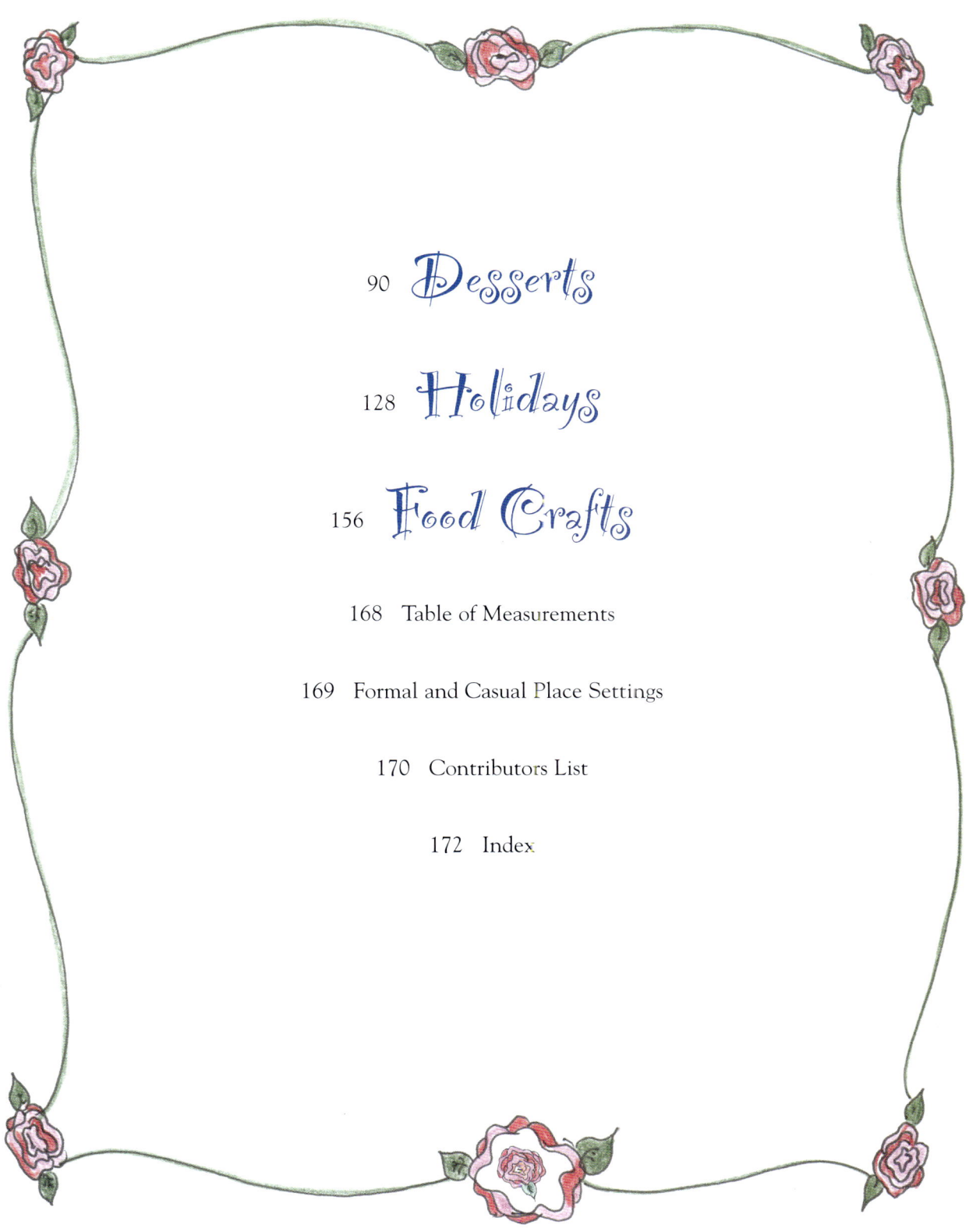

Cookbook Committee

Meredith Roberts
Cookbook Chair

Katie Powell
Text/Non-Recipe Chair

Vickie Hammer
Recipe Chair

Holly Short
Art & Design Chair

Angelina Bruno Pearson
Cookbook Illustrator

Cookbook Committee

Cookbook Chair
Meredith Roberts

Cookbook Marketing Assistants
Vickie Hammer
Katie Powell
Holly Short

Cookbook Business Manager
Debbie Matteucci

Sustaining Advisor
Mary Ann Cozby

President
Kristen Seeber

President Elect
Sandi Hegwood

Cookbook Illustrator
Angelina Bruno Pearson

The Junior League of Tyler, Inc.

The Mission

The Junior League of Tyler, Inc., is an organization of women committed to promoting voluntarism, developing the potential of women, and improving communities through the effective action and leadership of trained volunteers.

Its purpose is exclusively educational and charitable.

About the Junior League of Tyler

Our organization began in 1950 as the Tyler Service League and became the Junior League of Tyler, Inc., in 1960. Since its inception, more than four million dollars has been given back to the Tyler community through the League's projects and community efforts.

The League's primary fundraisers have consisted of the Bargain Box, which opened in 1950 and operated for numerous years; Mistletoe & Magic, our holiday market, which has been going strong for twenty-seven years; and we look forward to introducing *Ring Around the Rosie,* a cookbook for children. The League has published two other cookbooks. *Cooking Through Rose-Colored Glasses* was first published in 1975, and *And Roses for the Table* made its debut in 1997. Spring Sweep is the League's biannual rummage sale, which occurs on even-numbered years.

Over the years, the Junior League of Tyler, Inc., has played a key role in the development of such agencies as the Stewart Regional Blood Center, Tyler Museum of Art, Juvenile Attention Center, Smith County Child Advocacy programs, Hospice of East Texas, Discovery Science Place, Tyler/Smith County Crimestoppers, and our own Summer Reading Camp.

Community agencies that the Junior League of Tyler, Inc., has supported over the years are numerous and include our areas of priority: youth and family issues, arts and education, and health services. Countless hours of volunteer service are devoted by our membership as we go about furthering our mission in our community.

About the Illustrator

I dedicate my art to my late husband Jerimy A. Pearson, my three beautiful children, Trevor, 13, Madison, 9, and Christian, 5. I want to thank my family and those very close to me for their continued support and encouragement. I have lived in Tyler for three years since the death of my beloved husband Jerimy. I was honored to be chosen by the Junior League of Tyler to illustrate the children's cookbook. I am amazed at what a superb group of women can do for our community. Thank you for such a wonderful opportunity.

Kids Cook recipes are recipes with kids in mind to assemble by themselves, but adult supervision is always best. Some of these recipes do require assistance with baking in an oven or heating on the stovetop.

Snacks

Mud

Gelatin Jigglers

Popsicles

Frozen Banana Pops

Snack Mix

Puppy Chow

Chocolate Popcorn

Emma's Oyster Crackers

Animals "To Go"

Sugared Pie Crust Sticks

Soft Pretzels

Greek Bagel Sandwiches

Better than Ranch Dip

Frozen Slushies

Kid's Fruit Punch

Boston Malt

Mud

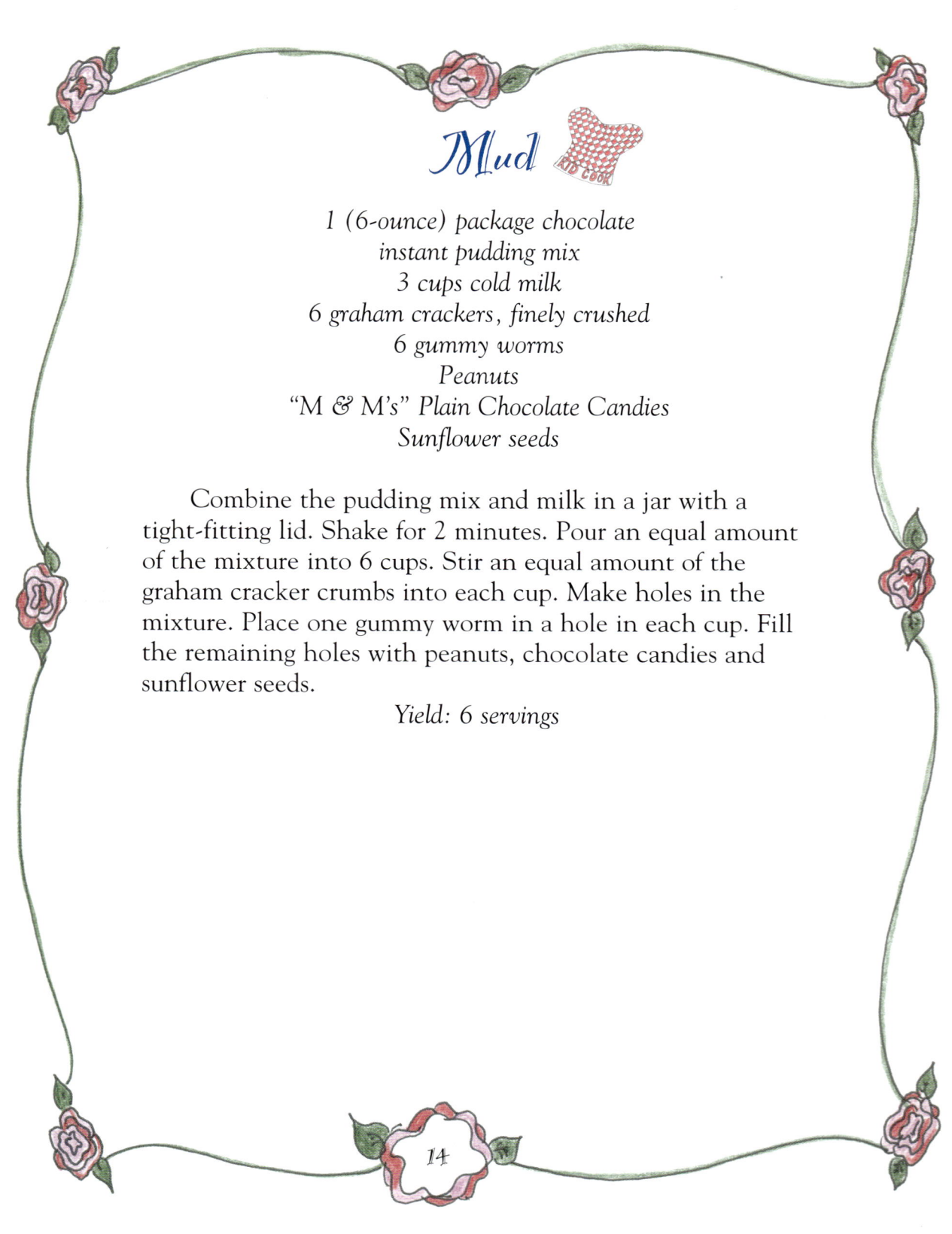

1 (6-ounce) package chocolate
instant pudding mix
3 cups cold milk
6 graham crackers, finely crushed
6 gummy worms
Peanuts
"M & M's" Plain Chocolate Candies
Sunflower seeds

Combine the pudding mix and milk in a jar with a tight-fitting lid. Shake for 2 minutes. Pour an equal amount of the mixture into 6 cups. Stir an equal amount of the graham cracker crumbs into each cup. Make holes in the mixture. Place one gummy worm in a hole in each cup. Fill the remaining holes with peanuts, chocolate candies and sunflower seeds.

Yield: 6 servings

Gelatin Jigglers

4 (4-ounce) packages, or 2 (8-ounce) packages
of your favorite flavor gelatin
2 1/2 cups boiling water

Combine the gelatin and water in a bowl and stir until
the gelatin is dissolved. Pour into a 9×13-inch pan. Chill for
3 hours or until firm. Cut the gelatin into your favorite shapes.

Yield: a variable amount

Popsicles

1 (3-ounce) package of your favorite flavor gelatin
1 envelope of your favorite flavor drink mix
1 cup sugar
2 cups boiling water
2 cups cold water

Combine the gelatin, drink mix, sugar and boiling water
in a bowl and stir until the gelatin, drink mix and sugar are
dissolved. Add the cold water. Pour into popsicle molds.
Freeze until firm.

Yield: 6 servings

Appetizers

When eating a formal meal or at a party, appetizers are served first. Some sample appetizers are shrimp cocktail, chips and dips or finger foods. Some appetizers require special utensils, some can be eaten with either a fork or a spoon and others may be picked up and eaten with your fingers. You should never take a chip or raw vegetable and return it to the dip after already biting off of it once— this is called "double-dipping."

Frozen Banana Pops

1 cup (6 ounces) chocolate chips
4 bananas, cut into halves
1 cup chopped nuts or granola

Place the chocolate chips in a microwave-safe bowl. Microwave on Low for 3 to 5 minutes or until melted and smooth, stirring every minute. Skewer each banana half with a wooden popsicle stick. Dip the bananas in the chocolate. Roll in the nuts. Place on a plate lined with waxed paper. Freeze for 2 hours or longer.

Yield: 8 servings

Snack Mix

2 cups Cheerios cereal
1 cup dry-roasted peanuts
1 cup "M & M's" Plain Chocolate Candies
1/2 cup each raisins, sunflower seeds and
butterscotch chips

Mix the cereal, peanuts, chocolate candies, raisins, sunflower seeds and butterscotch chips in a bowl. Store in an airtight container.

Yield: 4 1/2 cups

Puppy Chow

1 cup (6 ounces) chocolate chips
1/2 cup peanut butter
1 (12-ounce) box Crispix cereal
Confectioners' sugar

Combine the chocolate chips and peanut butter in a microwave-safe bowl. Microwave until melted and smooth, stirring frequently. You may also combine in a saucepan over simmering water and heat until melted and smooth, stirring frequently. Combine with the cereal in a bowl and mix gently. Add confectioners' sugar, stirring gently until the mixture is coated and dry.

Yield: about 14 cups

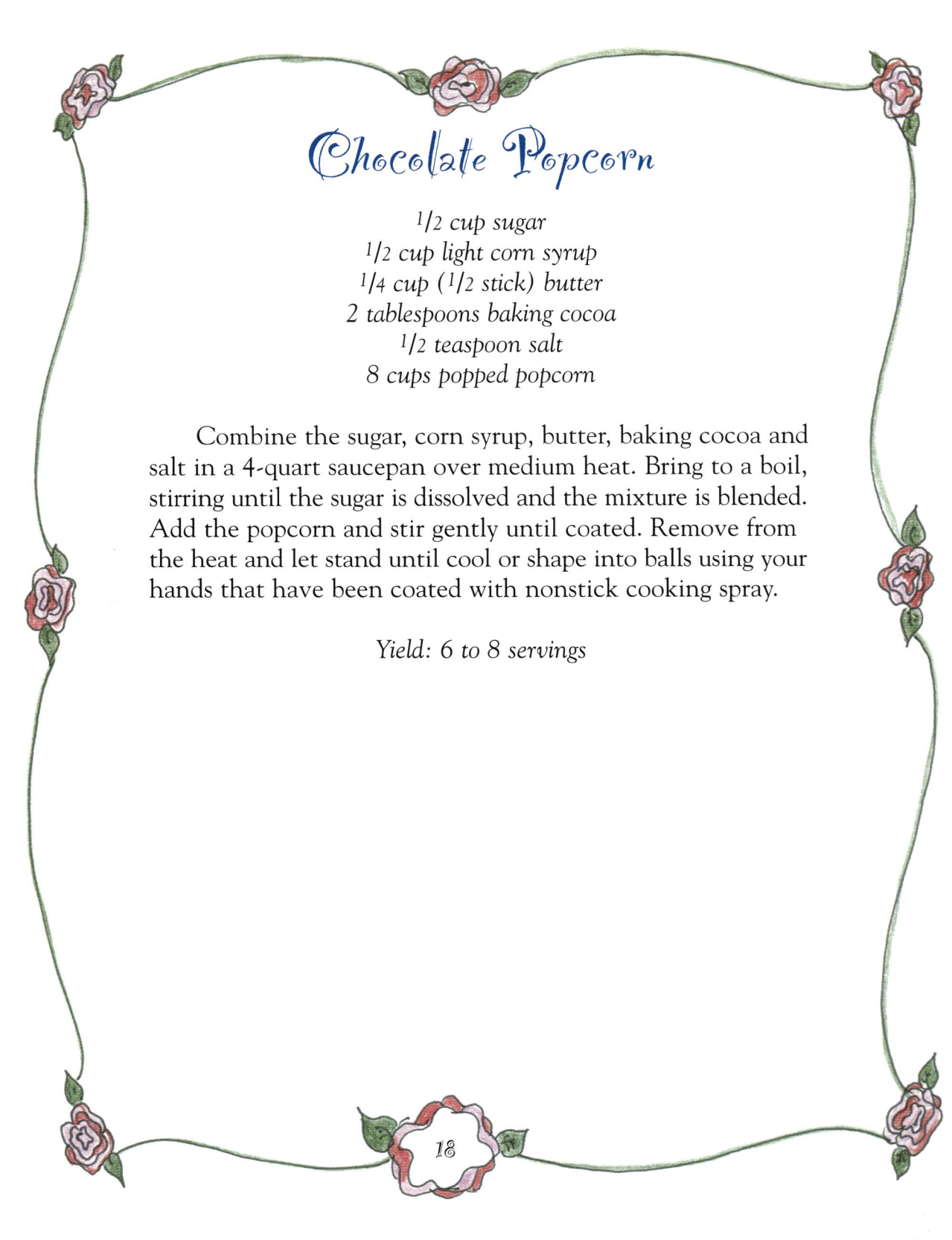

Chocolate Popcorn

¹/2 cup sugar
¹/2 cup light corn syrup
¹/4 cup (¹/2 stick) butter
2 tablespoons baking cocoa
¹/2 teaspoon salt
8 cups popped popcorn

Combine the sugar, corn syrup, butter, baking cocoa and salt in a 4-quart saucepan over medium heat. Bring to a boil, stirring until the sugar is dissolved and the mixture is blended. Add the popcorn and stir gently until coated. Remove from the heat and let stand until cool or shape into balls using your hands that have been coated with nonstick cooking spray.

Yield: 6 to 8 servings

Emma's
☆Oyster Crackers

2 (10-ounce) packages oyster crackers
3/4 cup vegetable oil
1 envelope ranch salad dressing mix
1/2 teaspoon dill weed
1/2 teaspoon lemon pepper
1/2 teaspoon garlic powder

Place the oyster crackers in a roasting pan. Combine the oil, salad dressing mix, dill weed, lemon pepper and garlic powder in a bowl and mix well. Pour over the crackers and stir gently until coated. Bake at 250 degrees for 15 to 20 minutes, stirring once after 10 minutes.

Yield: 20 servings

Animals "To Go"

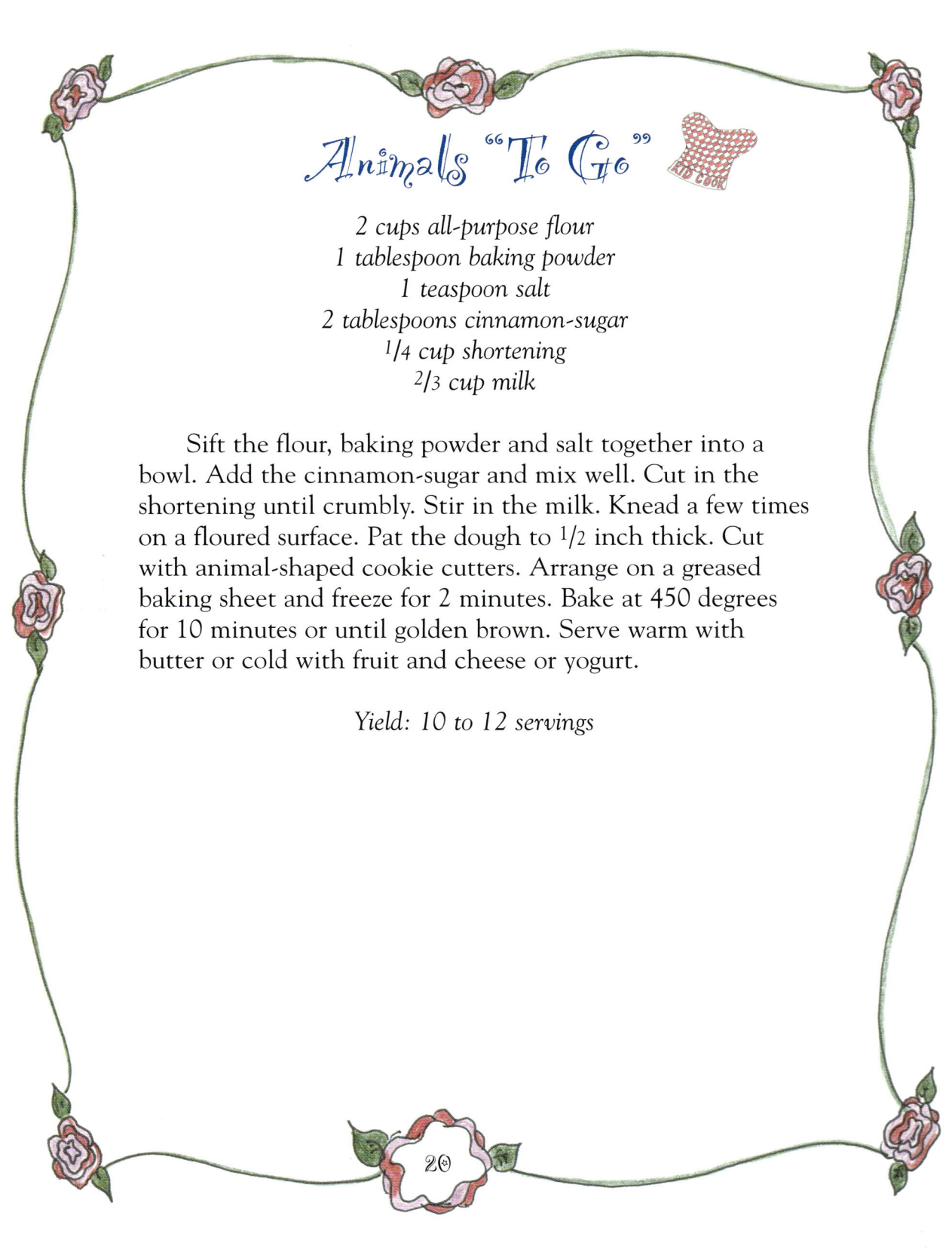

2 cups all-purpose flour
1 tablespoon baking powder
1 teaspoon salt
2 tablespoons cinnamon-sugar
1/4 cup shortening
2/3 cup milk

Sift the flour, baking powder and salt together into a bowl. Add the cinnamon-sugar and mix well. Cut in the shortening until crumbly. Stir in the milk. Knead a few times on a floured surface. Pat the dough to 1/2 inch thick. Cut with animal-shaped cookie cutters. Arrange on a greased baking sheet and freeze for 2 minutes. Bake at 450 degrees for 10 minutes or until golden brown. Serve warm with butter or cold with fruit and cheese or yogurt.

Yield: 10 to 12 servings

Sugared Pie Crust Sticks

1 (1-crust) pie pastry, at room temperature
Butter-flavored nonstick cooking spray
Cinnamon-sugar to taste

Cut the pie pastry into sticks or your favorite shapes. Spray with nonstick cooking spray. Sprinkle with cinnamon-sugar and arrange on a baking sheet. Bake at 425 degrees for 10 minutes. You may use colored sugar instead of cinnamon-sugar. For example, use red and green sugar for Christmas, red and blue sugar for the Fourth of July, red and pink sugar for Valentine's Day and pastel sugar for Easter.

Yield: 4 servings

Burps, Slurps, Sneezes and Coughs

If you burp, just say, "Excuse me." Do not giggle or make an issue of it. Do not slurp, smack your lips, or make any other annoying noises while dining. Turn away from the table to sneeze, cough, or blow your nose. For sneezing and coughing, cover your mouth with your hand. For nose blowing, use a tissue—never use your napkin.

Soft Pretzels

1 envelope fast-rising dry yeast
$1^1/3$ cups warm water
1 tablespoon sugar
$1/2$ teaspoon salt
$3^1/2$ to 4 cups all-purpose flour
1 egg
1 tablespoon water
2 tablespoons coarse salt

Sprinkle the yeast over $1^1/3$ cups water in a large bowl. Stir until the yeast is dissolved. Stir in the sugar, $1/2$ teaspoon salt and $3^1/2$ cups flour gradually until the dough is soft and slightly sticky. Knead on a floured surface for 2 to 3 minutes or until the dough is smooth and elastic, adding additional flour if necessary. Divide the dough into halves. Divide each half into six pieces. Roll each portion with floured hands into a 15-inch rope. Shape into pretzels and arrange on a baking sheet sprayed with nonstick cooking spray.

Combine the egg and 1 tablespoon water in a small bowl and mix well. Brush onto the pretzels. Sprinkle with the coarse salt. Bake at 375 degrees for 15 to 20 minutes or until golden brown.

Yield: 12 pretzels

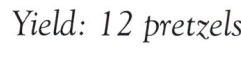

Greek Bagel Sandwiches

3 bagels, your favorite flavor
6 slices ham
6 slices Muenster cheese
6 slices tomato (optional)
Greek seasoning

Cut each bagel in half lengthwise. Arrange the bagel halves on a baking sheet. Layer each bagel half with a slice of ham, a slice of cheese and a slice of tomato. Sprinkle with Greek seasoning. Bake at 400 degrees until the cheese melts.

Yield: 6 servings

Better than Ranch Dip

1 cup mayonnaise
1 cup sour cream
1 tablespoon parsley
1 tablespoon chives
1 tablespoon dill seeds
1 teaspoon seasoned salt
1/4 teaspoon garlic salt
1/4 teaspoon onion salt

Combine the mayonnaise, sour cream, parsley, chives, dill seeds, seasoned salt, garlic salt and onion salt in a bowl and mix well. Chill, covered, for 30 minutes. Serve with your favorite vegetables and chips.

Yield: 2 cups

Frozen Slushies

1 package lime drink mix
64 ounces pineapple juice
4 cups water
2 cups sugar
2 liters ginger ale
Food coloring (optional)

Combine the drink mix, pineapple juice, water and sugar in a large plastic container and stir until the drink mix and the sugar are dissolved. Place the container in the freezer. Freeze for 4 to 12 hours. Remove from the freezer 20 to 30 minutes before ready to serve. Scoop the mixture into cups. Pour the ginger ale over the pineapple mixture and stir until slushy. Add a few drops of food coloring, if desired.

Yield: 20 servings

Courses

When you eat a formal meal, food is served in a certain order called courses.

First Course
Appetizer

Second Course
Soup

Third Course
Salad

Fourth Course
Fish or Sorbet

Main Course
Meat

Sixth Course
Dessert

Kid's Fruit Punch

2 (12-ounce) cans frozen orange juice concentrate
4 cups apple juice
1³/4 cups unsweetened pineapple juice

Prepare the orange juice in a large bowl using the package directions. Add the apple juice and pineapple juice and mix well. Chill until ready to serve.

Yield: 24 servings

Boston Malt

2 to 3 scoops vanilla ice cream
3/4 to 1 cup milk
2 to 3 tablespoons chocolate syrup
1 tablespoon malted milk powder

Scoop the ice cream into a tall glass. Fill 3/4 full with the milk. Add the chocolate syrup and sprinkle with the malted milk powder. Stir until blended.

Yield: 1 serving

Breakfast

Breakfast Pizza

Breakfast Casserole

Omelet in a Bag

Toad in a Hole

Sausage Cheese Balls

Puff Pancake

Swedish "Skinny" Pancakes

French Toast

Aunt Marilyn's Chocolate Gravy

Bubble Bread

Monkey Bread

Monkey's Favorite Banana Bread

Heavenly Cinnamon Loaves

Easy Cinnamon Roll

Madison's Marvelous Muffins

Breakfast Cookies

Breakfast Parfait

Fruity Smoothie

Orange Julius

Heavenly Hot Cocoa

Breakfast Pizza

1 package canned pizza dough
Margarine, softened
5 eggs, beaten
Salt and pepper to taste
1 cup (4 ounces) shredded Cheddar cheese
6 slices bacon, crisp-cooked and crumbled
Paprika to taste
Parsley to taste

Line a 10×15-inch baking pan with foil. Brush the pan with margarine. Press the pizza dough over the bottom of the prepared pan and brush with margarine. Pour the eggs over the pizza dough. Sprinkle with salt and pepper. Sprinkle with the cheese. Top with the bacon. Sprinkle with paprika and parsley. Bake at 400 degrees for 15 minutes. Cut into squares to serve. You may substitute crescent roll dough for the pizza dough, pressing the perforations to seal. You may substitute chopped ham for the bacon.

Yield: 10 to 12 servings

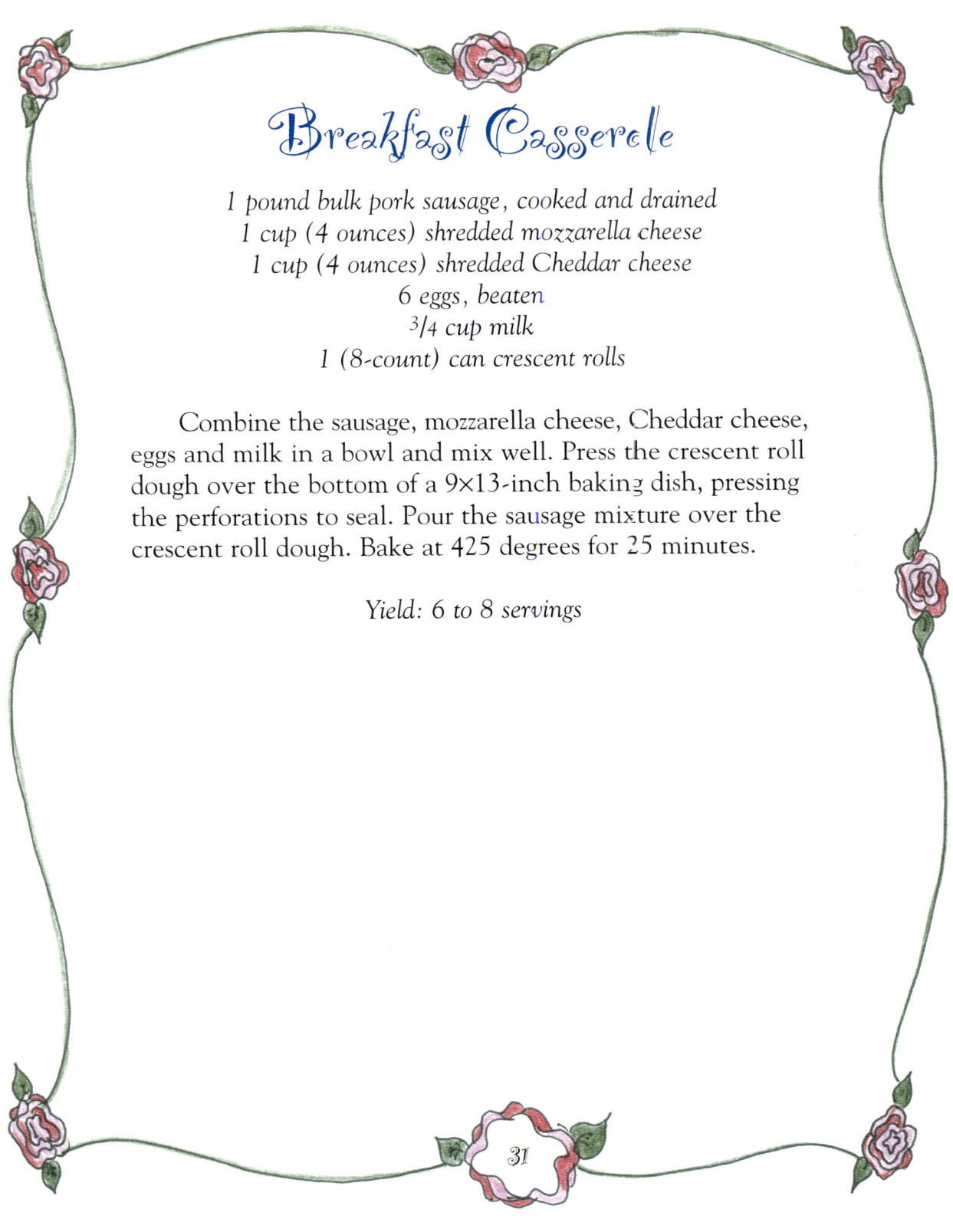

Breakfast Casserole

1 pound bulk pork sausage, cooked and drained
1 cup (4 ounces) shredded mozzarella cheese
1 cup (4 ounces) shredded Cheddar cheese
6 eggs, beaten
3/4 cup milk
1 (8-count) can crescent rolls

Combine the sausage, mozzarella cheese, Cheddar cheese, eggs and milk in a bowl and mix well. Press the crescent roll dough over the bottom of a 9×13-inch baking dish, pressing the perforations to seal. Pour the sausage mixture over the crescent roll dough. Bake at 425 degrees for 25 minutes.

Yield: 6 to 8 servings

Omelet in a Bag

1 to 2 eggs
Bacon bits to taste (optional)
Chopped onions, green bell peppers,
mushrooms and tomatoes to taste (optional)
Shredded cheese to taste (optional)
Chopped cooked ham or cooked bulk pork sausage
to taste (optional)
Salt and pepper to taste

Place the egg in a sealable plastic bag. Add the bacon bits, onions, bell peppers, mushrooms, tomatoes, cheese, ham, salt and pepper. Place the bag in boiling water to cover in a saucepan. Boil until the eggs are set. Remove the bag from the water and eat the omelet from the bag, if desired.

Yield: 1 serving

Toad in a Hole

1 teaspoon butter
1 slice bread
1 egg
Salt and pepper to taste

Melt the butter over low heat in a skillet. Cut a hole in the center of the bread, reserving the cut out center of bread. Place the bread in the skillet. Toast lightly on both sides. Place the egg in the hole in the bread. Cook the egg to the desired degree of doneness, turning once. Season with salt and pepper. Spread butter on both sides of the reserved circle of bread and toast lightly. Serve immediately.

Yield: 1 serving

Sausage Cheese Balls

1 pound bulk pork sausage
1 pound sharp Cheddar cheese, shredded
3 cups baking mix
1/2 cup water

Mix all the ingredients in a bowl with your hands. Shape into bite-size balls. Arrange on a baking sheet. Bake at 375 degrees for 10 to 15 minutes or until cooked through.

Yield: 24 to 36 sausage balls

During a Meal

sit up straight. Do not lounge all over the table. You may lean slightly forward over your plate when you eat, so that food doesn't land in your lap.

Puff Pancake

1/2 cup (1 stick) butter
1 cup all-purpose flour
1 cup milk
6 eggs, beaten
1/4 cup orange juice (optional)
1/2 cup sugar
Dash of salt

Melt the butter in a 9×13-inch baking dish in the oven. Combine the flour and milk in a bowl and mix well. Add the eggs, orange juice, sugar and salt and mix well. Pour into the prepared pan. Bake at 425 degrees for 20 minutes. Serve with confectioners' sugar or syrup.

Yield: 6 to 8 servings

34

Swedish "Skinny" Pancakes

1 1/2 cups milk
3 tablespoons butter
3 eggs, beaten
3/4 cup all-purpose flour
1/2 teaspoon salt
1/2 teaspoon vanilla extract

Heat the milk and butter in a saucepan over low heat until the butter is melted, stirring occasionally. Stir in the eggs. Sift in the flour and stir until the flour is dissolved. Add the salt and vanilla and mix well. Pour 1/4 cup of the batter at a time onto a hot, lightly greased nonstick griddle or skillet. Cook until golden brown on both sides, turning once. Serve immediately.

Yield: 3 to 4 servings

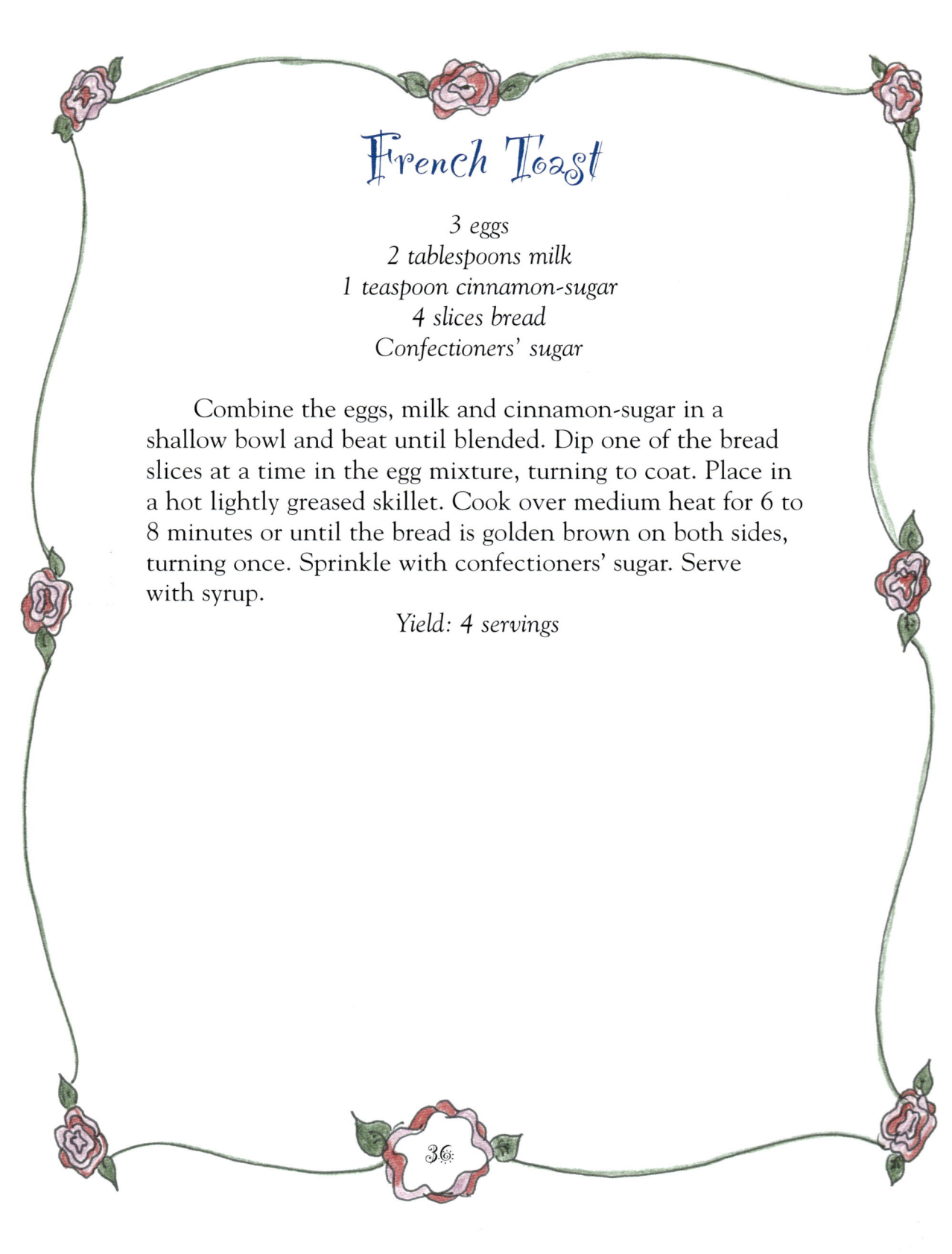

French Toast

3 eggs
2 tablespoons milk
1 teaspoon cinnamon-sugar
4 slices bread
Confectioners' sugar

Combine the eggs, milk and cinnamon-sugar in a shallow bowl and beat until blended. Dip one of the bread slices at a time in the egg mixture, turning to coat. Place in a hot lightly greased skillet. Cook over medium heat for 6 to 8 minutes or until the bread is golden brown on both sides, turning once. Sprinkle with confectioners' sugar. Serve with syrup.

Yield: 4 servings

Aunt Marilyn's Chocolate Gravy

1 tablespoon all-purpose flour
1 tablespoon baking cocoa
1/2 cup sugar
1 cup milk
1 teaspoon vanilla extract

Combine the flour, baking cocoa and sugar in a saucepan. Add the milk and vanilla and mix well. Bring to a boil over medium heat, stirring frequently. Serve over biscuits.

Yield: 2 cups

Bubble Bread

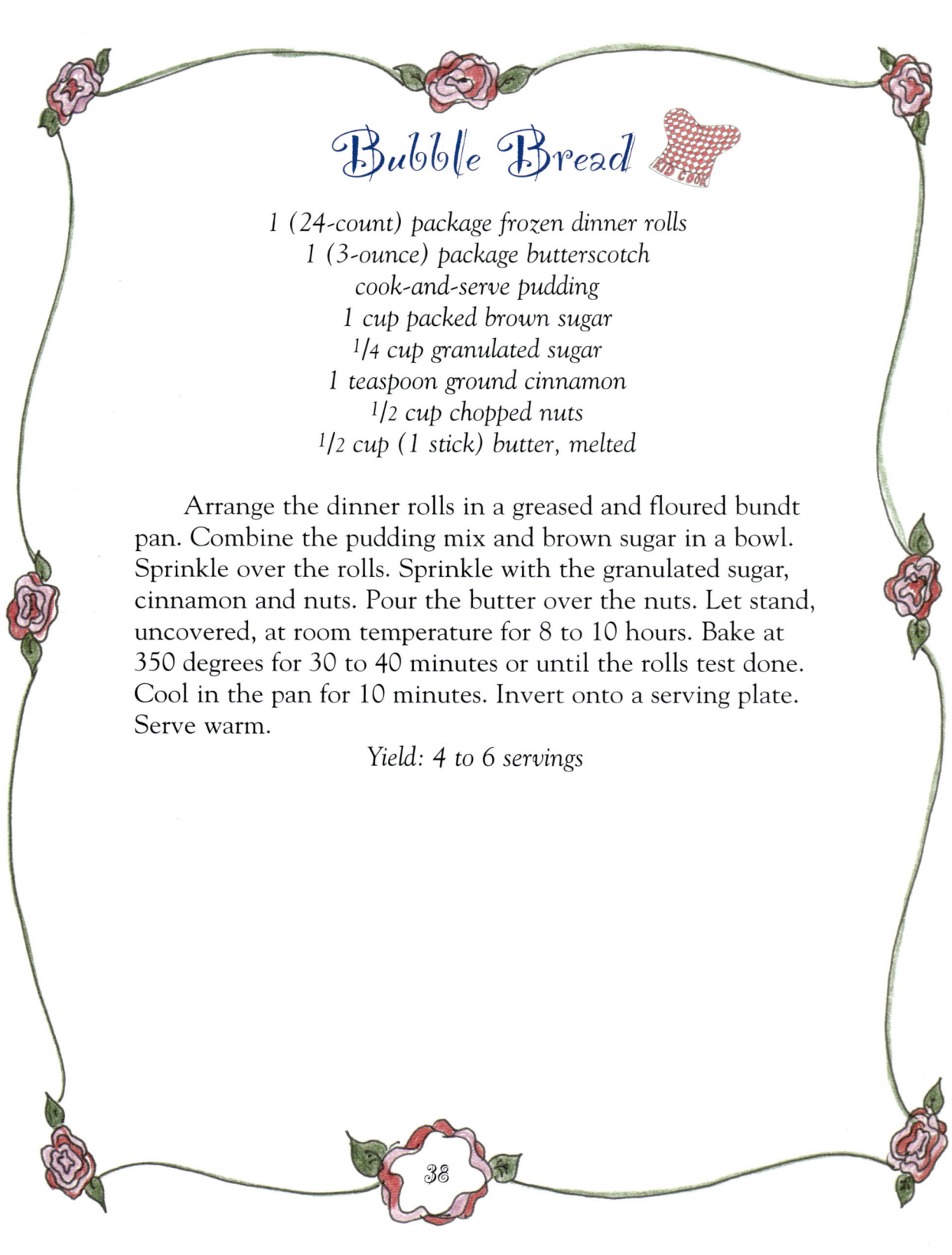

1 (24-count) package frozen dinner rolls
1 (3-ounce) package butterscotch
cook-and-serve pudding
1 cup packed brown sugar
1/4 cup granulated sugar
1 teaspoon ground cinnamon
1/2 cup chopped nuts
1/2 cup (1 stick) butter, melted

Arrange the dinner rolls in a greased and floured bundt pan. Combine the pudding mix and brown sugar in a bowl. Sprinkle over the rolls. Sprinkle with the granulated sugar, cinnamon and nuts. Pour the butter over the nuts. Let stand, uncovered, at room temperature for 8 to 10 hours. Bake at 350 degrees for 30 to 40 minutes or until the rolls test done. Cool in the pan for 10 minutes. Invert onto a serving plate. Serve warm.

Yield: 4 to 6 servings

Monkey Bread

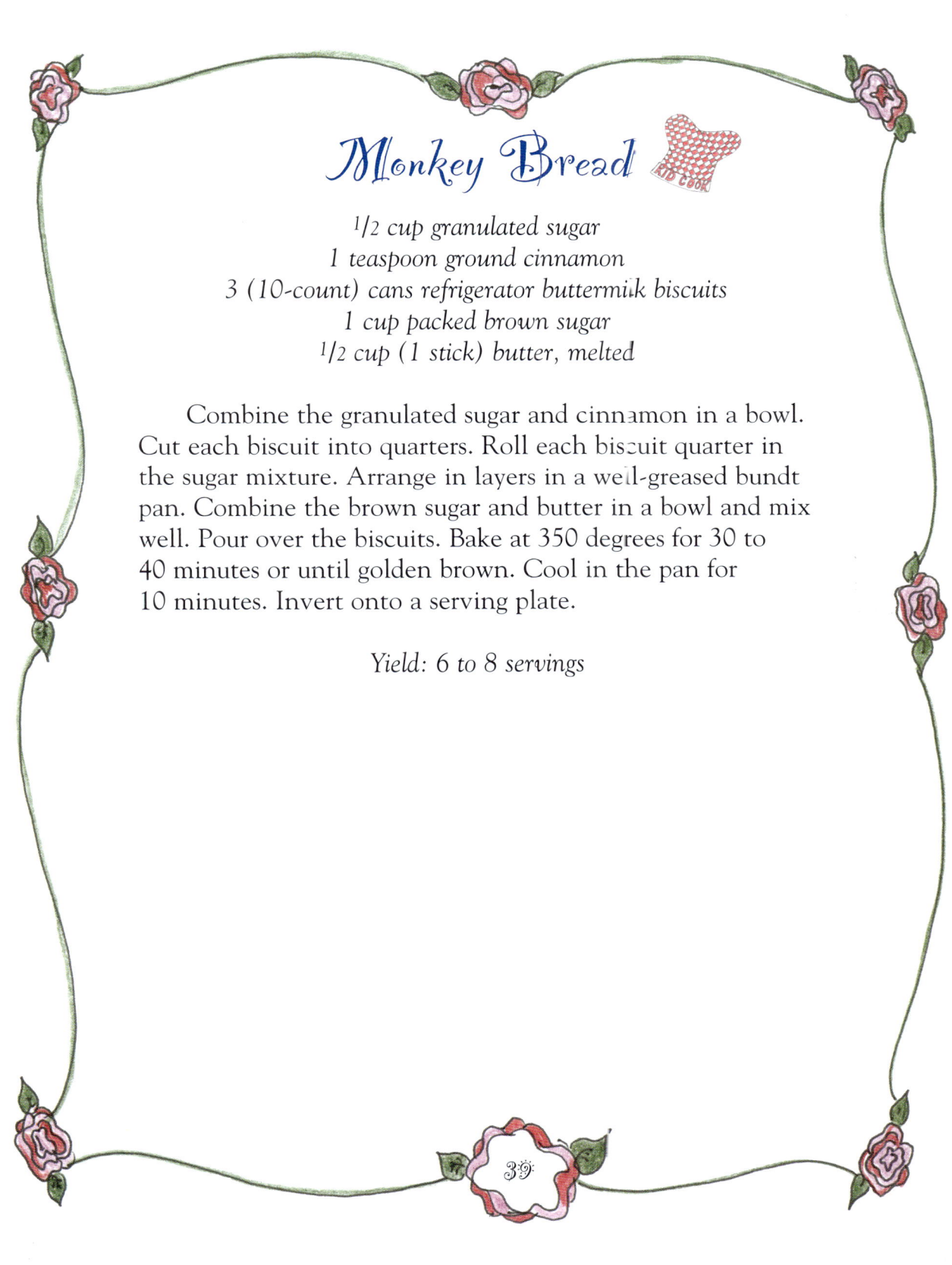

1/2 cup granulated sugar
1 teaspoon ground cinnamon
3 (10-count) cans refrigerator buttermilk biscuits
1 cup packed brown sugar
1/2 cup (1 stick) butter, melted

Combine the granulated sugar and cinnamon in a bowl. Cut each biscuit into quarters. Roll each biscuit quarter in the sugar mixture. Arrange in layers in a well-greased bundt pan. Combine the brown sugar and butter in a bowl and mix well. Pour over the biscuits. Bake at 350 degrees for 30 to 40 minutes or until golden brown. Cool in the pan for 10 minutes. Invert onto a serving plate.

Yield: 6 to 8 servings

Elbows

Elbows should never rest on the table. Elbows may be placed on the table only between courses, but it is not recommended. When cutting and eating your food, always keep your elbows relaxed at your sides. Do not stick them out like chicken wings—you'll look like you are trying to hatch an egg!

Monkey's Favorite Banana Bread

1 (2-layer) package yellow cake mix
4 ounces cream cheese, softened
2 eggs
3 ripe bananas, mashed

Combine the cake mix, cream cheese, eggs and bananas in a bowl and mix well. Spoon into a greased loaf pan. Bake at 350 degrees for 30 to 40 minutes or until a wooden pick inserted in the center comes out clean.

Yield: 8 to 10 servings

Heavenly Cinnamon Loaves

1 (2-layer) package yellow cake mix with pudding
4 eggs
3/4 cup each vegetable oil and water
1 teaspoon vanilla extract
1/2 cup sugar
3 tablespoons ground cinnamon

Combine the cake mix, eggs, oil, water and vanilla in a mixing bowl and beat for 3 minutes. Pour half the batter evenly into two greased and floured 4×8-inch disposable loaf pans. Combine the sugar and cinnamon in a bowl. Sprinkle half the sugar mixture evenly over the batter. Pour the remaining batter over the sugar mixture. Sprinkle evenly with the remaining sugar mixture. Swirl gently with a knife. Bake at 350 degrees for 45 minutes or until a wooden pick inserted in the center comes out clean. Cool in the pans on a wire rack. For miniature cinnamon loaves, pour half the batter evenly into five greased and floured 3×5-inch disposable loaf pans. Sprinkle evenly with the sugar mixture. Pour the remaining batter over the sugar mixture. Sprinkle with the remaining sugar mixture. Swirl gently with a knife. Bake at 350 degrees for 35 minutes or until the loaves test done.

Yield: 2 loaves or 5 miniature loaves

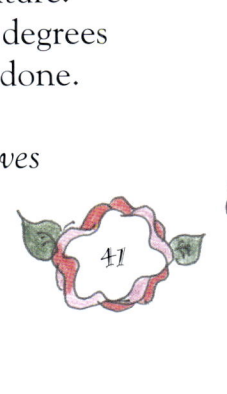

Easy Cinnamon Rolls

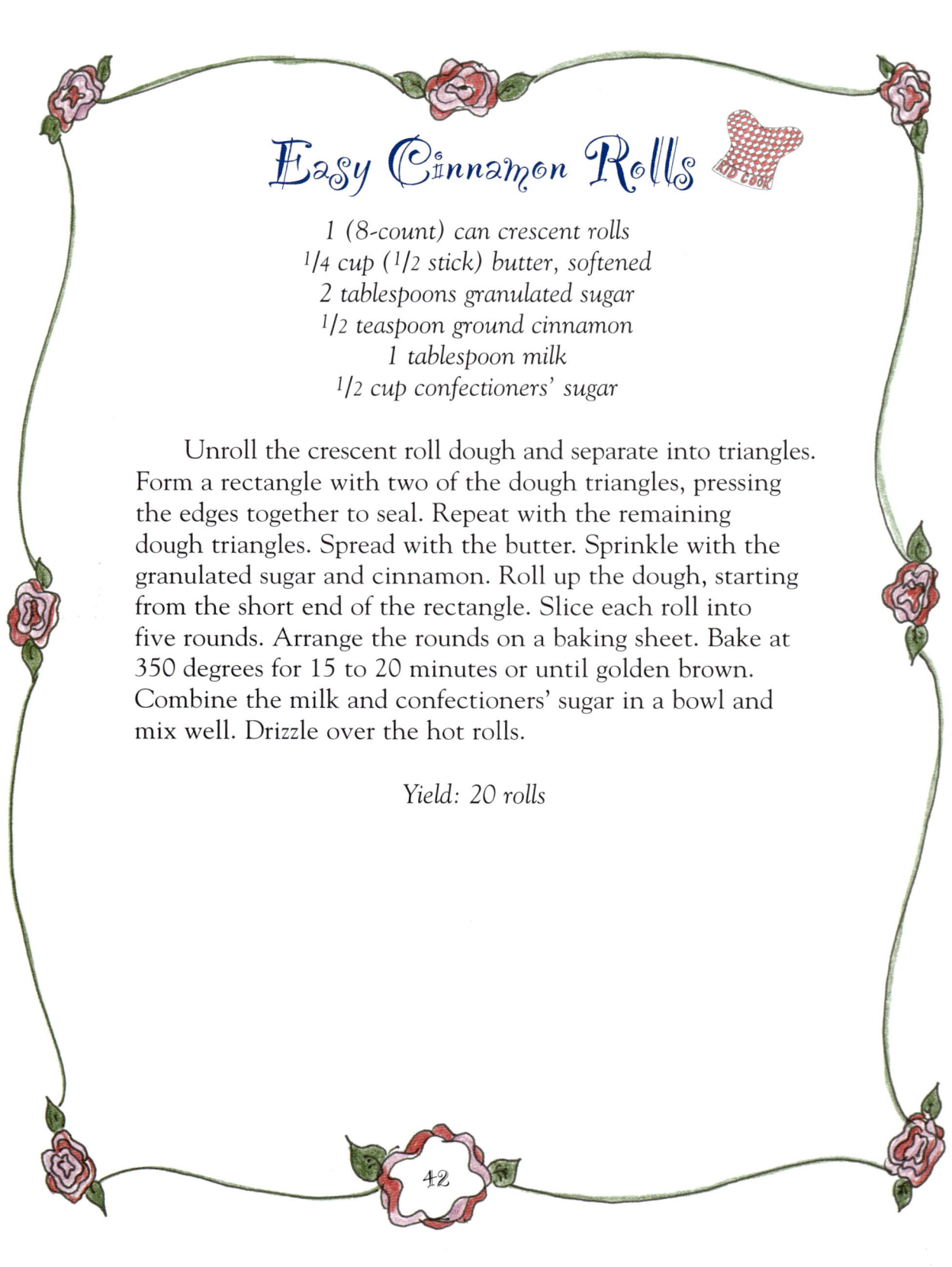

1 (8-count) can crescent rolls
1/4 cup (1/2 stick) butter, softened
2 tablespoons granulated sugar
1/2 teaspoon ground cinnamon
1 tablespoon milk
1/2 cup confectioners' sugar

Unroll the crescent roll dough and separate into triangles. Form a rectangle with two of the dough triangles, pressing the edges together to seal. Repeat with the remaining dough triangles. Spread with the butter. Sprinkle with the granulated sugar and cinnamon. Roll up the dough, starting from the short end of the rectangle. Slice each roll into five rounds. Arrange the rounds on a baking sheet. Bake at 350 degrees for 15 to 20 minutes or until golden brown. Combine the milk and confectioners' sugar in a bowl and mix well. Drizzle over the hot rolls.

Yield: 20 rolls

Madison's Marvelous Muffins

Streusel Topping
6 tablespoons all-purpose flour
6 tablespoons sugar
3 tablespoons butter or margarine, softened

Blueberry Muffins
1 tablespoon all-purpose flour
$1/2$ to 1 cup blueberries
$1^1/2$ cups all-purpose flour
$3/4$ cup sugar
2 teaspoons baking powder
$1/2$ teaspoon salt
$1/2$ cup milk
$1/4$ cup canola oil or vegetable oil
1 egg

For the topping, combine the flour and sugar in a bowl. Cut in the butter with a knife until crumbly.

For the muffins, combine 1 tablespoon flour and the blueberries in a bowl and toss gently to coat. Combine $1^1/2$ cups flour, the sugar, baking powder, salt, milk, canola oil and egg in a mixing bowl and beat until blended. Fold the blueberries in gently. Pour into lightly greased muffin cups. Sprinkle with the streusel topping. Bake at 400 degrees for 20 to 25 minutes or until the muffins test done.

Yield: 10 muffins

Breakfast Cookies

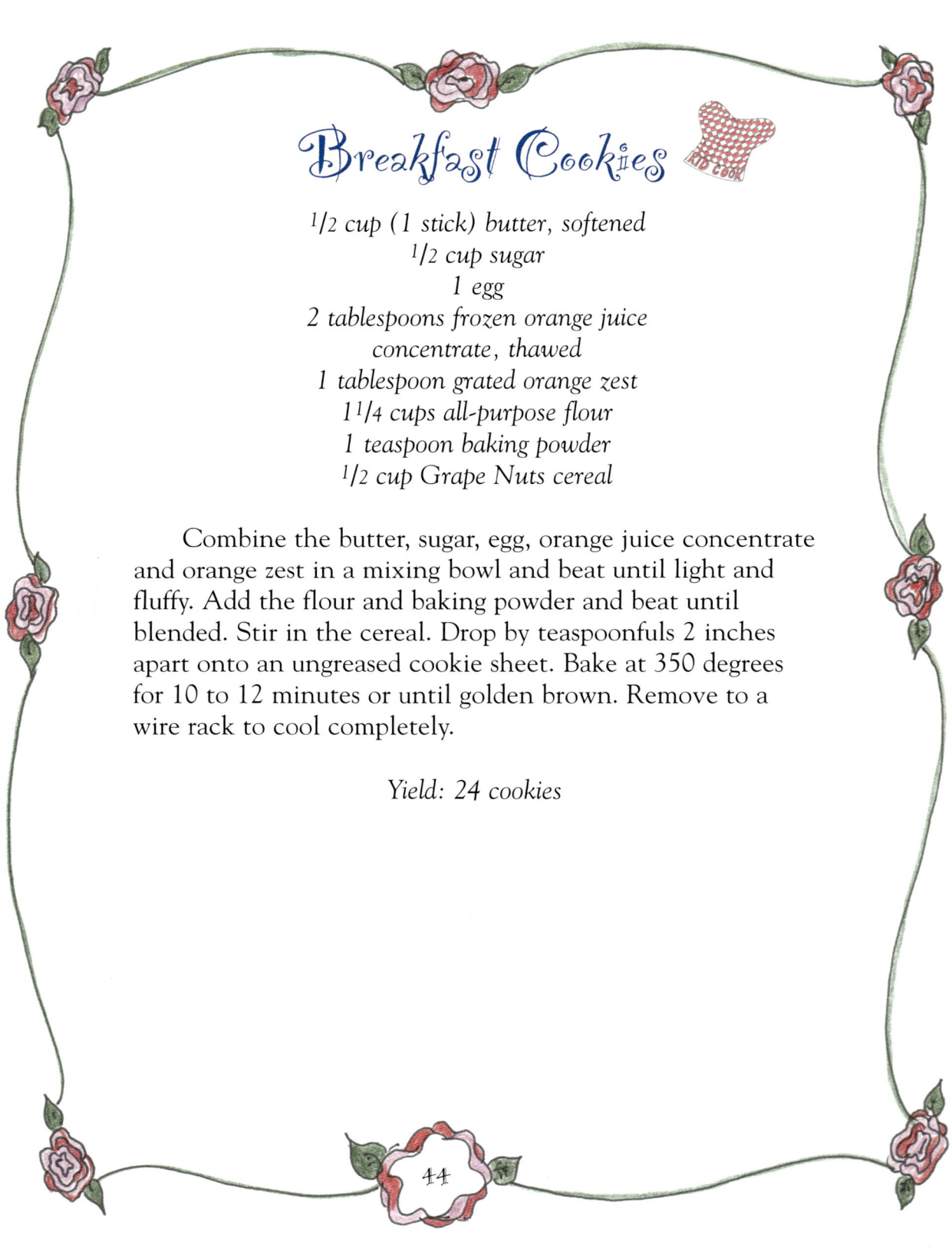

1/2 cup (1 stick) butter, softened
1/2 cup sugar
1 egg
2 tablespoons frozen orange juice
concentrate, thawed
1 tablespoon grated orange zest
1 1/4 cups all-purpose flour
1 teaspoon baking powder
1/2 cup Grape Nuts cereal

Combine the butter, sugar, egg, orange juice concentrate and orange zest in a mixing bowl and beat until light and fluffy. Add the flour and baking powder and beat until blended. Stir in the cereal. Drop by teaspoonfuls 2 inches apart onto an ungreased cookie sheet. Bake at 350 degrees for 10 to 12 minutes or until golden brown. Remove to a wire rack to cool completely.

Yield: 24 cookies

Breakfast Parfait

24 ounces of your favorite flavor yogurt
1 cup granola
12 ounces of your choice fresh fruit
such as strawberries, bananas, blueberries,
blackberries or raspberries

Layer 2 to 3 tablespoons yogurt, 1 tablespoon granola and 1 to 2 tablespoons fruit in each of four parfait glasses. Repeat the layers two or three more times.

Yield: 4 servings

Fruity Smoothie

1 cup milk
1 cup vanilla ice cream or fruit-flavored ice cream
2 tablespoons honey
1 cup of your favorite frozen fruit

Place the milk, ice cream, honey and fruit in a blender. Process on high until smooth. Pour into two glasses and serve immediately.

Yield: 2 servings

Finger Bowl

A finger bowl is sometimes served with the dessert course. After eating dessert, dip your fingertips, one hand at a time, into the bowl. Dry them on your napkin. You may touch your fingers to your lips, and then pat them dry with your napkin. You should do it gracefully—remember you are not taking a bath!

Orange Julius

*1 (6-ounce) container frozen
orange juice concentrate
1 cup milk
1/2 cup sugar
1 cup water
1/2 teaspoon vanilla extract
12 ice cubes*

Place the orange juice concentrate, milk, sugar, water, vanilla and ice cubes in a blender. Process until smooth. Pour into glasses and serve immediately.

Yield: 8 servings

Heavenly Hot Cocoa

11 cups powdered milk
2 pounds confectioners' sugar
16 ounces non-dairy powdered creamer
16 ounces chocolate drink mix
2 (6-ounce) packages chocolate
instant pudding mix

Place the powdered milk in a roasting pan. Add the confectioners' sugar, creamer, drink mix and pudding mix one at a time, mixing well with a large spoon after each addition. Store in airtight jars or tins. Great to use as gifts for friends, teachers and neighbors. To prepare a cup of cocoa, fill a mug half full with the cocoa mix. Add boiling water to fill the mug and mix well. Top with miniature marshmallows or whipped cream.

Yield: makes enough cocoa mix for
about six 20-ounce containers

Main Dishes

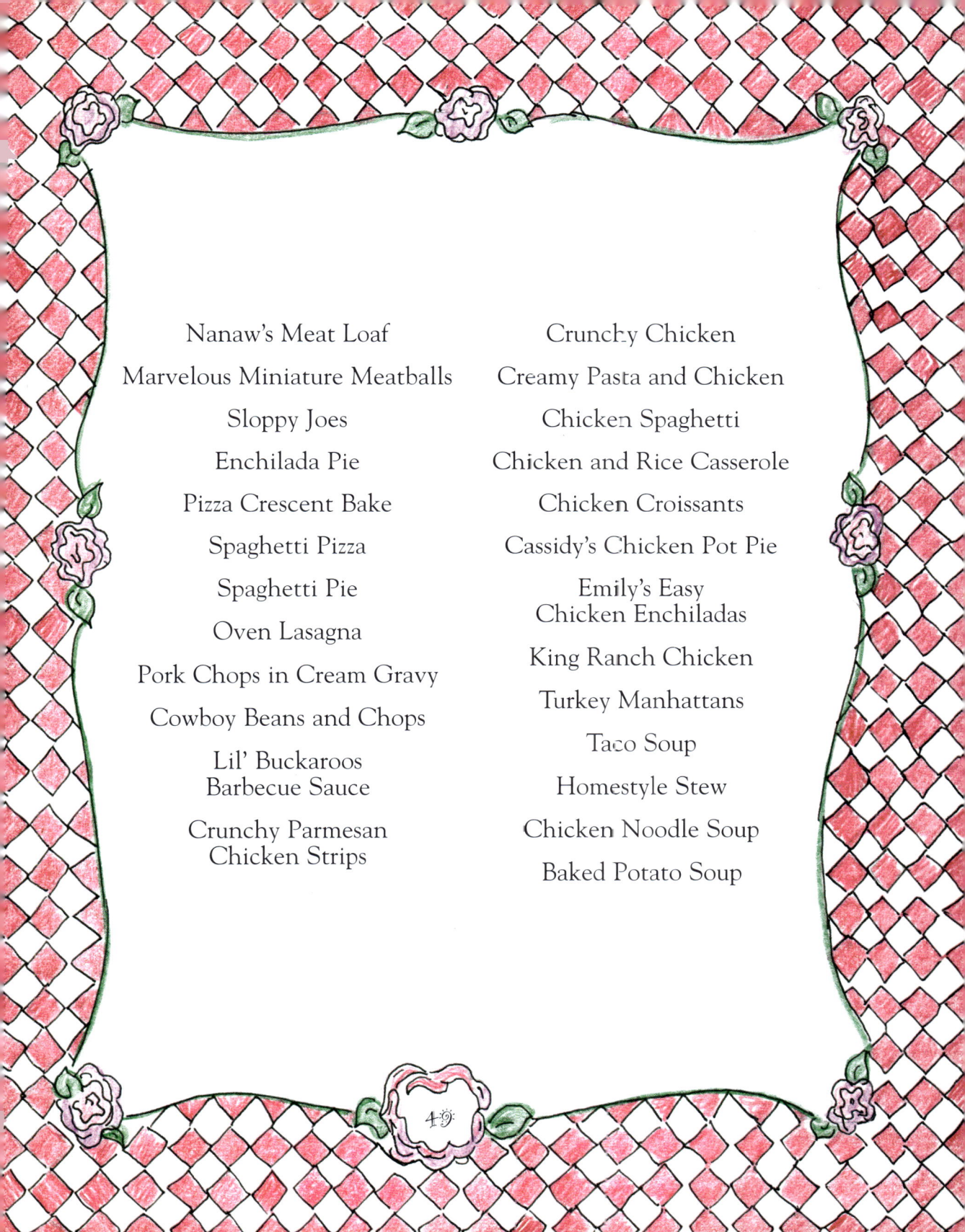

Nanaw's Meat Loaf

Marvelous Miniature Meatballs

Sloppy Joes

Enchilada Pie

Pizza Crescent Bake

Spaghetti Pizza

Spaghetti Pie

Oven Lasagna

Pork Chops in Cream Gravy

Cowboy Beans and Chops

Lil' Buckaroos
Barbecue Sauce

Crunchy Parmesan
Chicken Strips

Crunchy Chicken

Creamy Pasta and Chicken

Chicken Spaghetti

Chicken and Rice Casserole

Chicken Croissants

Cassidy's Chicken Pot Pie

Emily's Easy
Chicken Enchiladas

King Ranch Chicken

Turkey Manhattans

Taco Soup

Homestyle Stew

Chicken Noodle Soup

Baked Potato Soup

Nanaw's Meat Loaf

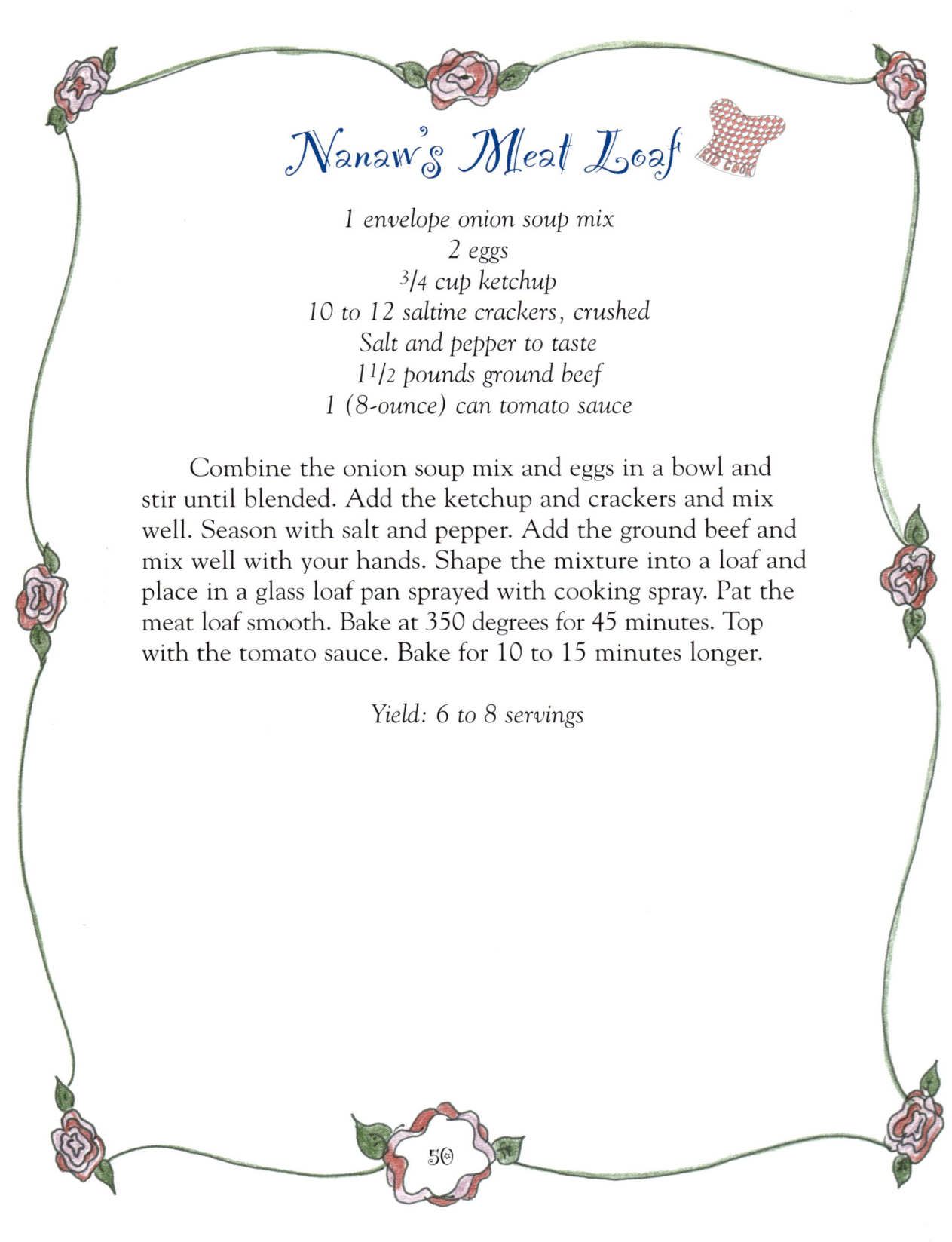

1 envelope onion soup mix
2 eggs
3/4 cup ketchup
10 to 12 saltine crackers, crushed
Salt and pepper to taste
1 1/2 pounds ground beef
1 (8-ounce) can tomato sauce

Combine the onion soup mix and eggs in a bowl and stir until blended. Add the ketchup and crackers and mix well. Season with salt and pepper. Add the ground beef and mix well with your hands. Shape the mixture into a loaf and place in a glass loaf pan sprayed with cooking spray. Pat the meat loaf smooth. Bake at 350 degrees for 45 minutes. Top with the tomato sauce. Bake for 10 to 15 minutes longer.

Yield: 6 to 8 servings

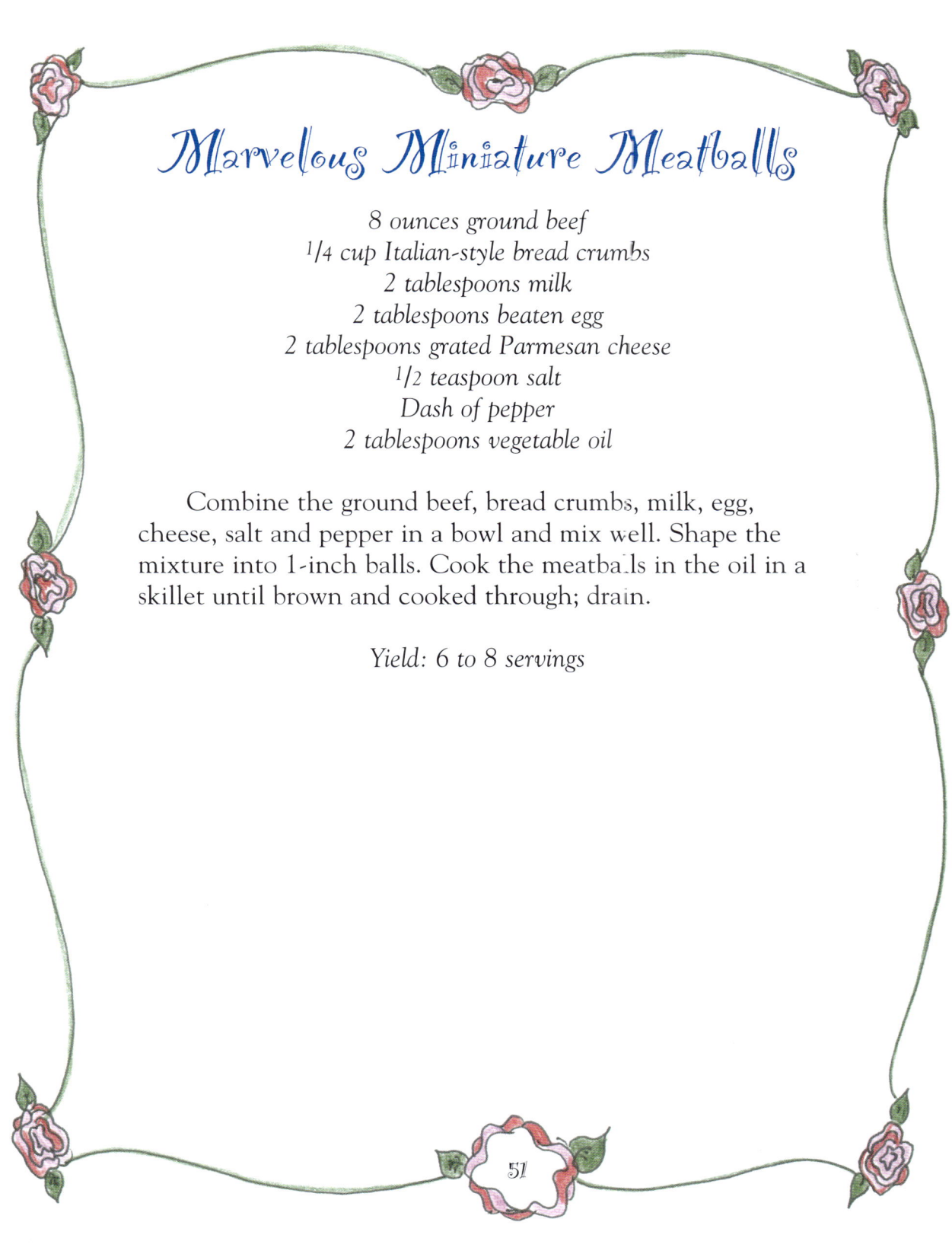

Marvelous Miniature Meatballs

8 ounces ground beef
1/4 cup Italian-style bread crumbs
2 tablespoons milk
2 tablespoons beaten egg
2 tablespoons grated Parmesan cheese
1/2 teaspoon salt
Dash of pepper
2 tablespoons vegetable oil

Combine the ground beef, bread crumbs, milk, egg, cheese, salt and pepper in a bowl and mix well. Shape the mixture into 1-inch balls. Cook the meatballs in the oil in a skillet until brown and cooked through; drain.

Yield: 6 to 8 servings

Garnish

It is okay to eat all of the pretty vegetables, fruits, and greens used to decorate your plate. If you have a lemon that needs to be squeezed over your food, it is best to hold the lemon wedge in one hand while you cup the other hand around it. That way you won't squirt your dinner partner!

Sloppy Joes

2 pounds ground beef
1 teaspoon garlic salt
1 teaspoon onion salt
Pepper to taste
1 cup ketchup
1/4 cup packed brown sugar
1 teaspoon yellow mustard or
spicy brown mustard

Brown the ground beef with the garlic salt, onion salt and pepper in a skillet, stirring until the ground beef is crumbly; drain. Add the ketchup, brown sugar and mustard and mix well. Simmer over low heat for 5 minutes, stirring occasionally. Spoon onto sandwich buns.

Yield: 8 to 10 servings

Enchilada Pie

1 pound ground beef
1 onion, chopped
1 tablespoon chili powder
1^1/2 teaspoons salt
^{1}/4 teaspoon pepper
1 (8-ounce) can tomato sauce
12 corn tortillas
1^1/2 cups (6 ounces) shredded Cheddar cheese
1 cup water

Brown the ground beef with the onion in a skillet, stirring until the ground beef is crumbly; drain. Stir in the chili powder, salt, pepper and tomato sauce. Alternate layers of the tortillas and ground beef mixture in a baking dish. Top with the cheese. Pour the water over the cheese layer. Bake, covered, at 400 degrees for 20 minutes.

Yield: 4 to 6 servings

53

Pizza Crescent Bake

2 (8-count) cans crescent rolls
1 pound ground beef
1 (15-ounce) can pizza sauce
1 cup (4 ounces) shredded Cheddar cheese
1 cup (4 ounces) shredded mozzarella cheese

Unroll 1 can of the crescent roll dough. Place over the bottom of a lightly greased 9×13-inch baking dish, pressing the perforations to seal. Brown the ground beef in a skillet, stirring until crumbly; drain. Sprinkle the ground beef over the dough. Pour the pizza sauce over the ground beef. Sprinkle with the Cheddar cheese and mozzarella cheese. Unroll the remaining can of crescent roll dough. Place over the cheese layer, pressing the perforations to seal. Bake at 350 degrees for 30 minutes or until golden brown.

Yield: 6 to 8 servings

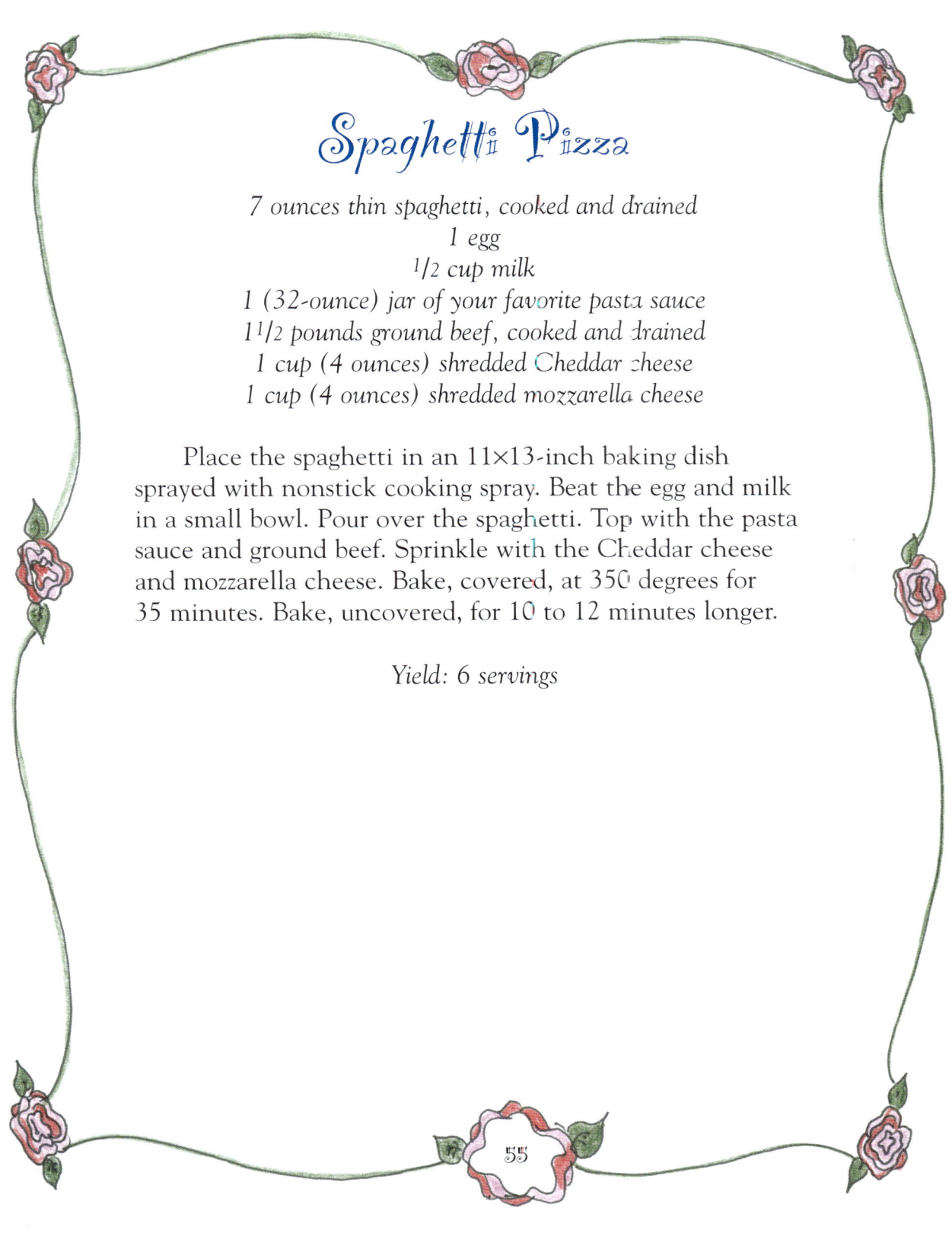

Spaghetti Pizza

7 ounces thin spaghetti, cooked and drained
1 egg
1/2 cup milk
1 (32-ounce) jar of your favorite pasta sauce
1 1/2 pounds ground beef, cooked and drained
1 cup (4 ounces) shredded Cheddar cheese
1 cup (4 ounces) shredded mozzarella cheese

Place the spaghetti in an 11×13-inch baking dish sprayed with nonstick cooking spray. Beat the egg and milk in a small bowl. Pour over the spaghetti. Top with the pasta sauce and ground beef. Sprinkle with the Cheddar cheese and mozzarella cheese. Bake, covered, at 350 degrees for 35 minutes. Bake, uncovered, for 10 to 12 minutes longer.

Yield: 6 servings

Spaghetti Pie

2 eggs
1/4 cup (1 ounce) grated Parmesan cheese
8 ounces thin spaghetti, cooked and drained
1/2 cup chopped green bell pepper
1/3 cup chopped onion
2 tablespoons butter
1 cup sour cream
1 pound ground Italian sausage
1 cup water
1 (6-ounce) can tomato paste
1 cup (4 ounces) shredded mozzarella cheese

Beat the eggs and Parmesan cheese in a medium bowl. Add the warm spaghetti and toss to combine. Arrange the spaghetti mixture over the bottom of a greased 10-inch pie plate to form a crust. Sauté the bell pepper and onion in the butter in a large skillet for 5 minutes. Stir in the sour cream. Spoon the mixture over the spaghetti layer. Brown the sausage in a saucepan over medium heat, stirring until crumbly; drain. Stir in the water and tomato paste. Reduce the heat and simmer for 10 minutes, stirring occasionally. Spoon the sausage mixture over the sour cream mixture. Bake, covered with foil, at 350 degrees for 25 to 30 minutes. Remove the foil and sprinkle with the mozzarella cheese. Bake, uncovered, for 3 to 5 minutes longer or until the cheese melts. Let stand for 10 minutes before slicing.

Yield: 6 to 8 servings

Oven Lasagna

1 pound ground beef
1 pound ground Italian sausage
1/4 teaspoon garlic salt
1/4 teaspoon onion salt
Dash of salt
Dash of pepper
2 (26-ounce) jars of your favorite pasta sauce
1 (8-ounce) box oven-ready lasagna noodles
2 cups (8 ounces) shredded
Cheddar/mozzarella cheese mixture
2 cups (8 ounces) shredded mozzarella cheese
1 cup (4 ounces) grated Parmesan cheese

Brown the ground beef and ground Italian sausage with the garlic salt, onion salt, salt and pepper in a skillet, stirring until the ground beef and sausage are crumbly; drain. Reduce the heat. Add the pasta sauce and mix well. Spoon some of the meat mixture over the bottom of a 9×13-inch baking dish. Top with two or three lasagna noodles. Sprinkle with some of the cheese. Continue the layering process, ending with the meat mixture and the cheeses. Bake at 350 degrees for 30 to 45 minutes or until heated through and bubbly.

Yield: 8 to 10 servings

Holding Flatware

Hold your flatware gracefully. You aren't using a shovel! You should hold them like you hold your pencil. The right hand is the "worker hand," and the left hand is the "helper hand." The right hand does the cutting and the feeding into your mouth, while the left hand stabilizes the food. If you are left handed, the left hand does the cutting and the right hand stabilizes the food. Don't stab your food with your fork. Never bang or click your flatware on the table or on your plate or bowl.

Pork Chops in Cream Gravy

6 (4-ounce) boneless center-cut loin pork chops or
bone-in breakfast pork chops
1/2 teaspoon salt
1 1/2 tablespoons butter
5 tablespoons all-purpose flour
2 cups 1% milk
1/2 teaspoon salt
1/2 teaspoon poultry seasoning
1/2 teaspoon black pepper

Sprinkle the pork chops with 1/2 teaspoon salt. Heat a large nonstick skillet over medium-high heat. Add the butter to the skillet and heat until melted, stirring constantly. Cook the pork chops in the butter for 3 minutes on each side. Remove the pork chops to a platter and keep warm. Add the flour to the drippings in the skillet. Whisk in the milk. Whisk in 1/2 teaspoon salt, the poultry seasoning and pepper. Return the pork chops to the skillet. Reduce the heat and cook, covered, for 7 minutes or until the gravy is thick and the pork chops are cooked through.

Yield: 6 servings

Cowboy Beans and Chops

4 to 6 thinly sliced bone-in pork chops
Salt and pepper to taste
1 (28-ounce) can of your favorite baked beans
1/2 cup ketchup
2 tablespoons brown sugar

Season the pork chops with salt and pepper. Pour the beans into a greased 9×13-inch baking dish. Arrange the pork chops over the beans. Combine the ketchup and brown sugar in a small bowl and mix well. Pour the ketchup mixture over the pork chops. Bake at 350 degrees for 30 to 40 minutes or until the pork chops are cooked through.

Yield: 4 to 6 servings

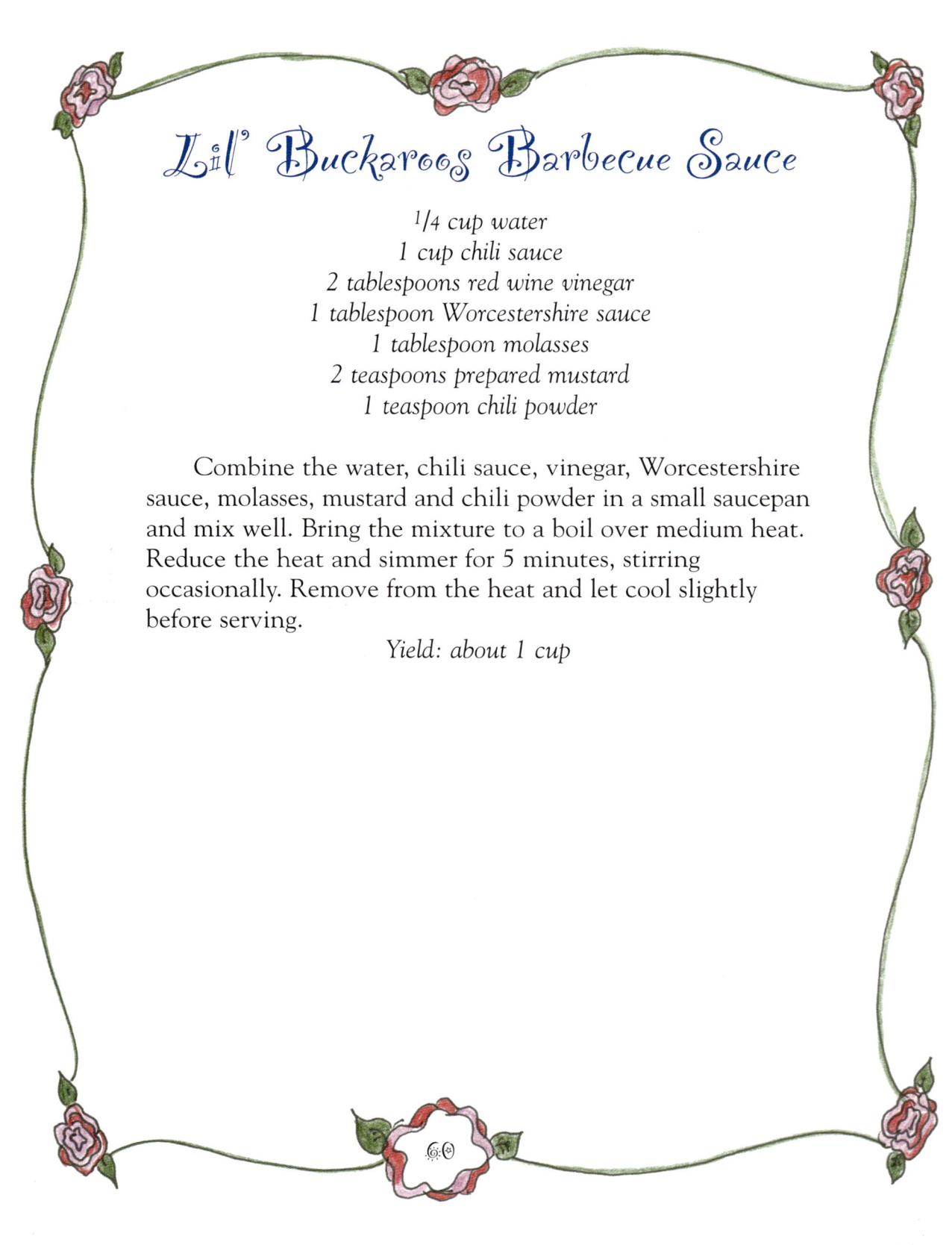

Lil' Buckaroos Barbecue Sauce

1/4 cup water
1 cup chili sauce
2 tablespoons red wine vinegar
1 tablespoon Worcestershire sauce
1 tablespoon molasses
2 teaspoons prepared mustard
1 teaspoon chili powder

Combine the water, chili sauce, vinegar, Worcestershire sauce, molasses, mustard and chili powder in a small saucepan and mix well. Bring the mixture to a boil over medium heat. Reduce the heat and simmer for 5 minutes, stirring occasionally. Remove from the heat and let cool slightly before serving.

Yield: about 1 cup

Crunchy Parmesan Chicken Strips

1 1/2 cups crushed seasoned croutons
1/2 cup (2 ounces) freshly grated Parmesan cheese
1 teaspoon parsley
1/2 teaspoon garlic salt
2 egg whites
1 tablespoon water
1 pound chicken tenders
1/2 cup ranch salad dressing

Combine the crushed croutons, cheese, parsley and garlic salt in a shallow bowl. Whisk the egg whites and water in a shallow bowl. Dip the chicken in the egg mixture. Roll in the crouton mixture to coat. Arrange the chicken on a baking sheet. Bake at 450 degrees for 15 minutes or until the chicken is cooked through. Serve with the salad dressing.

Yield: 4 to 6 servings

Interesting Conversation

Having interesting and lively conversation is the last ingredient of an excellent meal. Mealtime, especially dinnertime, is the time to relax and enjoy good food and the company of your family and friends.

Turn off the television—share your thoughts, listen to one another, tell what you have learned today, and ask questions.

Crunchy Chicken

2 cups crushed butter crackers
3/4 cup (3 ounces) grated Parmesan cheese
1/4 cup chopped fresh parsley
2 teaspoons salt
1/8 teaspoon pepper
1/2 teaspoon garlic salt or minced garlic
4 to 6 boneless chicken breasts
1 cup (2 sticks) butter, melted

Combine the crushed crackers, cheese, parsley, salt, pepper and garlic salt in a shallow bowl. Dip the chicken breasts in the butter. Roll in the cracker mixture to coat. Arrange in a baking dish sprayed with nonstick cooking spray. Bake at 350 degrees for 30 minutes or until cooked through.

Yield: 4 to 6 servings

Creamy Pasta and Chicken

4 chicken breasts, chopped
1 tablespoon olive oil
Salt and pepper to taste
1 (10-ounce) can cream of chicken soup
1 1/4 cups milk
1/4 cup (1 ounce) grated Parmesan cheese
1 (3-ounce) can French-fried onions
2 cups cooked penne or rigatoni

Cook the chicken in the olive oil in a skillet until golden brown and cooked through. Season with salt and pepper. Stir in the soup, milk, cheese, half the onions and the pasta. Cook over low heat until heated through. Sprinkle with the remaining onions. Garnish with chopped tomatoes, if desired.

Yield: 6 to 8 servings

Take an interest in those around you! Of course, you should use an inside voice when dining in. Don't talk while food is in your mouth. Always swallow your food first, and then talk. If you are asked a question while you have too much food in your mouth, you may have to wait to reply until you finish chewing and swallowing. In turn, try not to ask a question of someone when he or she has just put food into his or her mouth.

63

Chicken Spaghetti

1 whole chicken
1 onion, chopped
1 bell pepper, chopped
3 tablespoons butter
2 (10-ounce) cans cream of mushroom soup
1 pound Velveeta cheese, cut into cubes
16 ounces spaghetti, cooked and drained

Boil the chicken in water to cover in a stockpot until the chicken is cooked through. Remove the chicken and reserve the broth. Chop the chicken, discarding the skin and bones. Sauté the onion and bell pepper in the butter in a large skillet. Add the soup and 2 mushroom soup cans of the reserved broth. Add the cheese and chicken and mix well. Simmer until the cheese melts and the mixture is heated through. Add the spaghetti and cook until heated through.

Yield: 8 to 10 servings

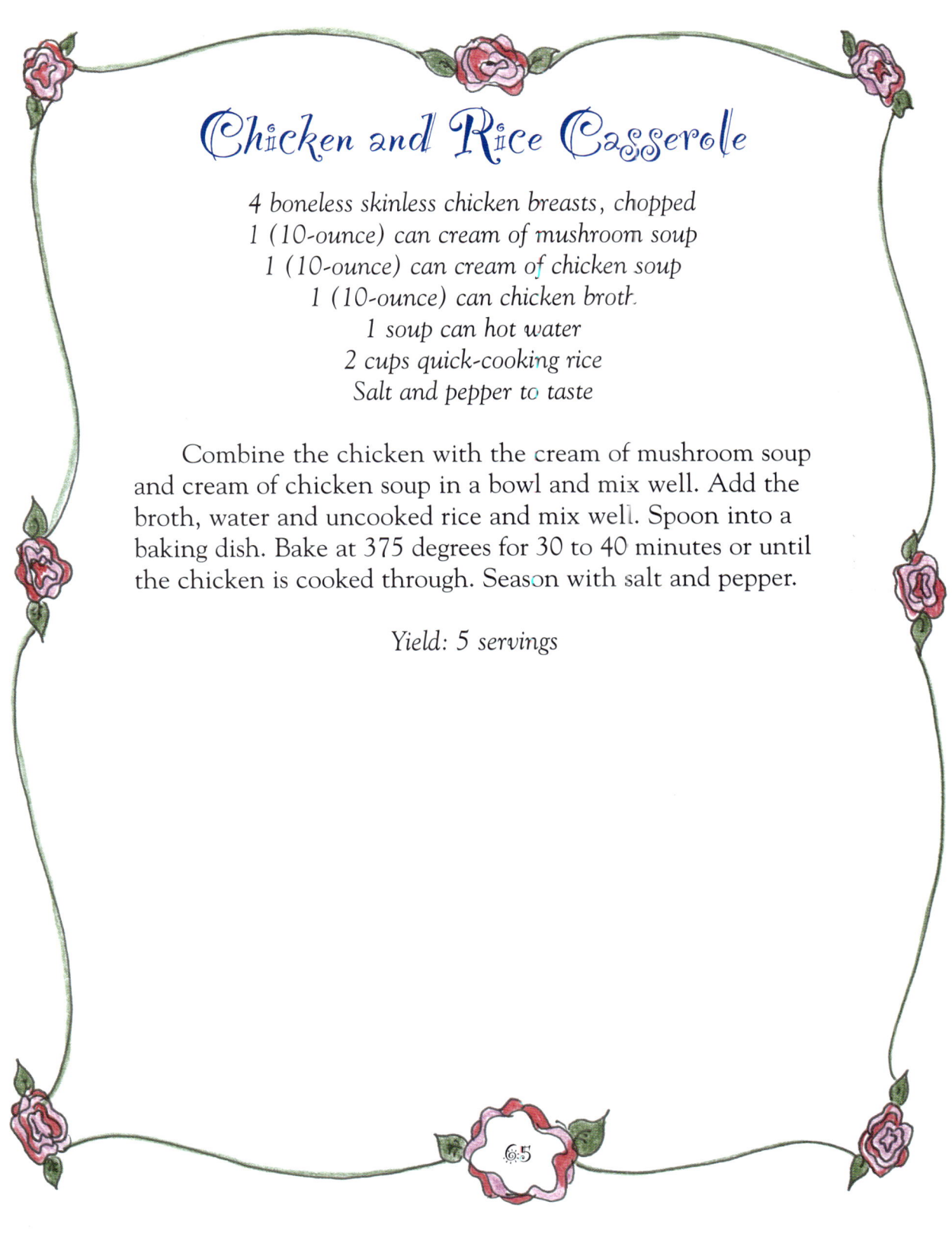

Chicken and Rice Casserole

4 boneless skinless chicken breasts, chopped
1 (10-ounce) can cream of mushroom soup
1 (10-ounce) can cream of chicken soup
1 (10-ounce) can chicken broth
1 soup can hot water
2 cups quick-cooking rice
Salt and pepper to taste

Combine the chicken with the cream of mushroom soup and cream of chicken soup in a bowl and mix well. Add the broth, water and uncooked rice and mix well. Spoon into a baking dish. Bake at 375 degrees for 30 to 40 minutes or until the chicken is cooked through. Season with salt and pepper.

Yield: 5 servings

Jelly

Jelly and butter should be put on your bread and butter plate. When the bread or rolls are passed to you, take one and place it on your bread and butter plate. Use the serving knife on the butter dish to get some butter and the spoon in the jelly dish to serve yourself jelly. If the table is set without the bread and butter service, put the bread on the side of your dinner plate. You should use your own dinner knife to spread your butter and jelly. Bread should be buttered and jellied one bite at a time.

Chicken Croissants

3 ounces cream cheese, softened
1^1/2 tablespoons margarine, softened
2 tablespoons milk
^{1}/4 teaspoon salt
^{1}/8 teaspoon pepper
2 cups chopped cooked chicken
1 tablespoon chopped onion
1 (8-count) can crescent rolls
1^1/2 tablespoons margarine, melted
^{3}/4 cup crushed seasoned croutons

Mix the cream cheese, 1^1/2 tablespoons margarine, the milk, salt and pepper in a bowl until smooth. Add the chicken and onion and mix well. Unroll the crescent roll dough and separate into triangles. Form a rectangle with two of the dough triangles, pinching the edges together to seal. Spoon some of the chicken mixture in the middle of the rectangle. Fold the sides of the dough over the chicken. Brush with melted butter and place on a baking sheet. Sprinkle with some of the crushed croutons. Repeat the procedure until all of the remaining ingredients are used. Bake at 350 degrees for 20 minutes.

Yield: 4 servings

66

Cassidy's Chicken Potpie

2 cups chopped cooked chicken
2 (10-ounce) cans cream of potato soup
1 (16-ounce) can mixed vegetables, drained
1/2 cup milk
1/2 teaspoon thyme
1/2 teaspoon pepper
1/4 teaspoon salt
1 (2-crust) pie pastry
1 egg, slightly beaten (optional)

Combine the chicken, soup, vegetables, milk, thyme, pepper and salt in a bowl and mix well. Line a greased 9-inch pie plate with one of the pie pastries. Spoon the chicken mixture over the pie pastry. Place the remaining pie pastry over the chicken mixture, sealing the edge with a fork. Brush with the egg. Bake, loosely covered with foil, at 375 degrees for 30 minutes. Remove the foil and bake an additional 10 minutes. Let cool for 10 minutes before serving. You may use your favorite cookie cutters to cut patterns in the top pie pastry before placing it over the chicken mixture, if desired.

Yield: 4 to 6 servings

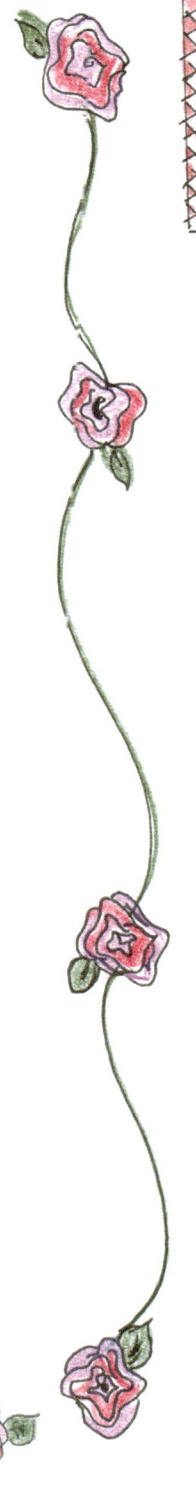

Emily's Easy
Chicken Enchiladas

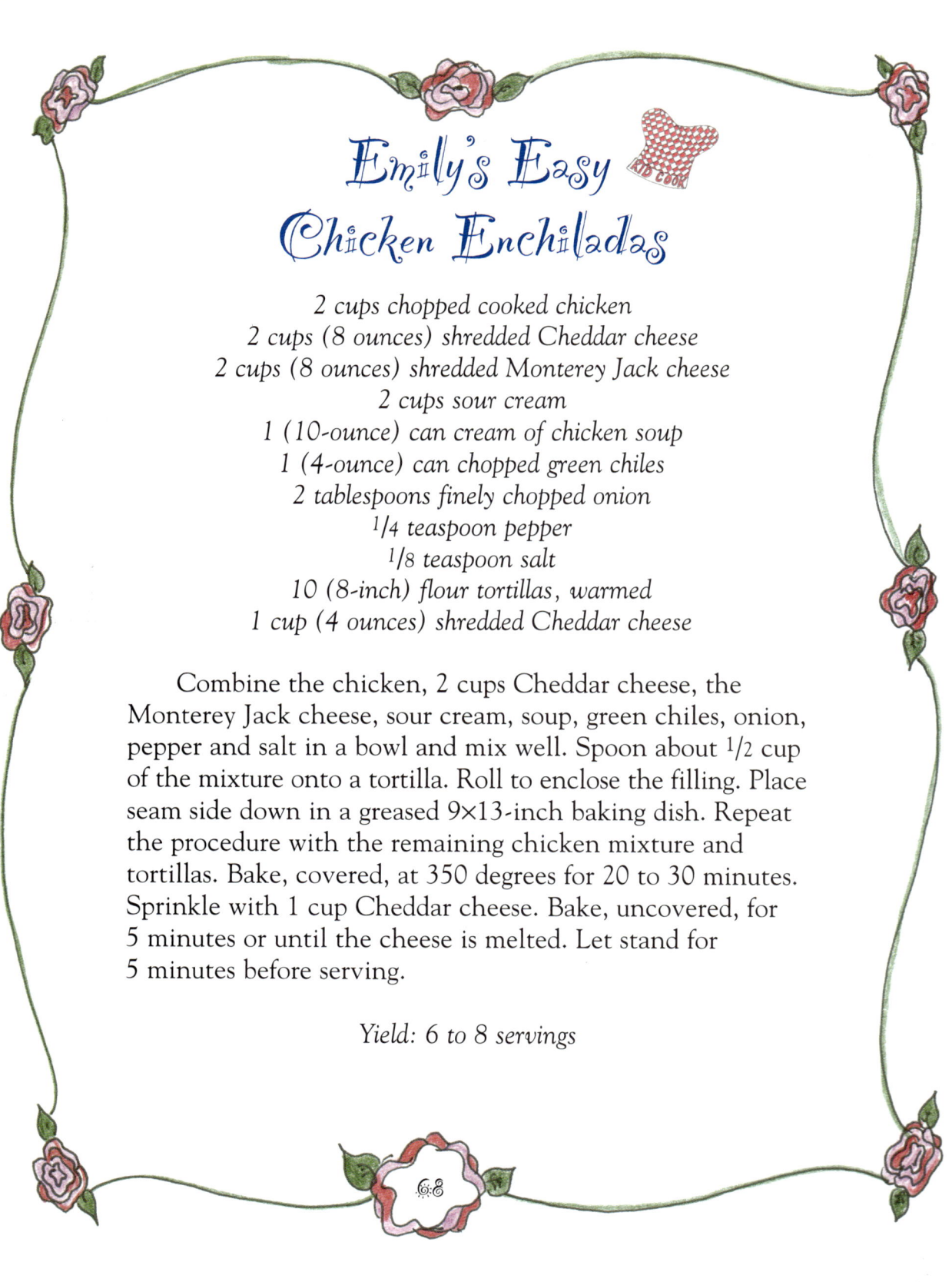

2 cups chopped cooked chicken
2 cups (8 ounces) shredded Cheddar cheese
2 cups (8 ounces) shredded Monterey Jack cheese
2 cups sour cream
1 (10-ounce) can cream of chicken soup
1 (4-ounce) can chopped green chiles
2 tablespoons finely chopped onion
1/4 teaspoon pepper
1/8 teaspoon salt
10 (8-inch) flour tortillas, warmed
1 cup (4 ounces) shredded Cheddar cheese

Combine the chicken, 2 cups Cheddar cheese, the
Monterey Jack cheese, sour cream, soup, green chiles, onion,
pepper and salt in a bowl and mix well. Spoon about 1/2 cup
of the mixture onto a tortilla. Roll to enclose the filling. Place
seam side down in a greased 9×13-inch baking dish. Repeat
the procedure with the remaining chicken mixture and
tortillas. Bake, covered, at 350 degrees for 20 to 30 minutes.
Sprinkle with 1 cup Cheddar cheese. Bake, uncovered, for
5 minutes or until the cheese is melted. Let stand for
5 minutes before serving.

Yield: 6 to 8 servings

King Ranch Chicken

2 chickens
1 (10-ounce) can cream of mushroom soup
1 (10-ounce) can chicken broth
1 (14-ounce) can diced tomatoes and green chiles
1/2 onion, finely chopped
12 corn tortillas
4 cups (16 ounces) shredded Cheddar cheese
1 teaspoon chili pepper

Boil the chicken in water to cover in a large saucepan for 45 minutes. Let stand until cool. Chop the chicken, discarding the skin and bones. Combine the soup, broth and tomatoes with green chiles in a saucepan. Cook over low heat until heated through, stirring occasionally. Arrange six of the tortillas in a greased 9×13-inch baking dish. Layer half the chicken, half the onion, half the soup mixture and half the cheese over the tortillas. Repeat the layers. Sprinkle with the chili pepper. Bake, covered with foil, at 350 degrees for 45 minutes. Remove the foil and bake, uncovered, for 15 minutes longer.

Yield: 12 servings

Turkey Manhattans

3 cups chopped cooked turkey
3 cups turkey broth or chicken broth
3 to 4 tablespoons flour
1/4 to 1/2 cup cold water
Salt and pepper to taste

Cook the turkey in the broth in a saucepan over medium-low heat until stringy. Blend the flour and water in a jar and add to the turkey. Cook until thickened, stirring constantly. Season with salt and pepper. Serve over mashed potatoes or buttered bread.

Yield: 8 servings

Taco Soup

2 pounds lean ground beef, browned and drained
1 (14-ounce) can stewed tomatoes
1 (14-ounce) can diced tomatoes and green chiles
1 (8-ounce) can Mexicorn
2 (16-ounce) cans ranch-style beans
1 (2-ounce) can chopped green chiles
1 package taco seasoning
1 teaspoon onion powder

Mix all the ingredients in a slow cooker. Cook on Low for 3 to 4 hours.

Yield: 8 servings

Homestyle Stew

1 to 2 pounds beef stew meat
1 large onion, chopped
2 tablespoons vegetable oil
Salt and pepper to taste
6 to 8 beef bouillon cubes
5 to 6 potatoes, peeled and chopped
1 (14-ounce) can Italian-style stewed tomatoes
1 (8-ounce) can carrots
2 (8-ounce) cans whole kernel corn
1 (16-ounce) can green beans
1 (8-ounce) can tomato sauce
2 teaspoons minced garlic
1 teaspoon seasoned salt, or to taste

Cook the beef and onion in the oil in a large stockpot until the beef is brown. Season with salt and pepper. Add water to cover and the bouillon cubes. Cook over medium heat for 3 to 4 hours or until the beef is cooked through and tender, stirring occasionally and adding water as needed. Add the potatoes, undrained tomatoes, undrained carrots, undrained corn, undrained green beans, tomato sauce, garlic and seasoned salt and mix well. Cook over medium heat for 30 to 45 minutes or until the potatoes are cooked through.

Yield: 8 to 10 servings

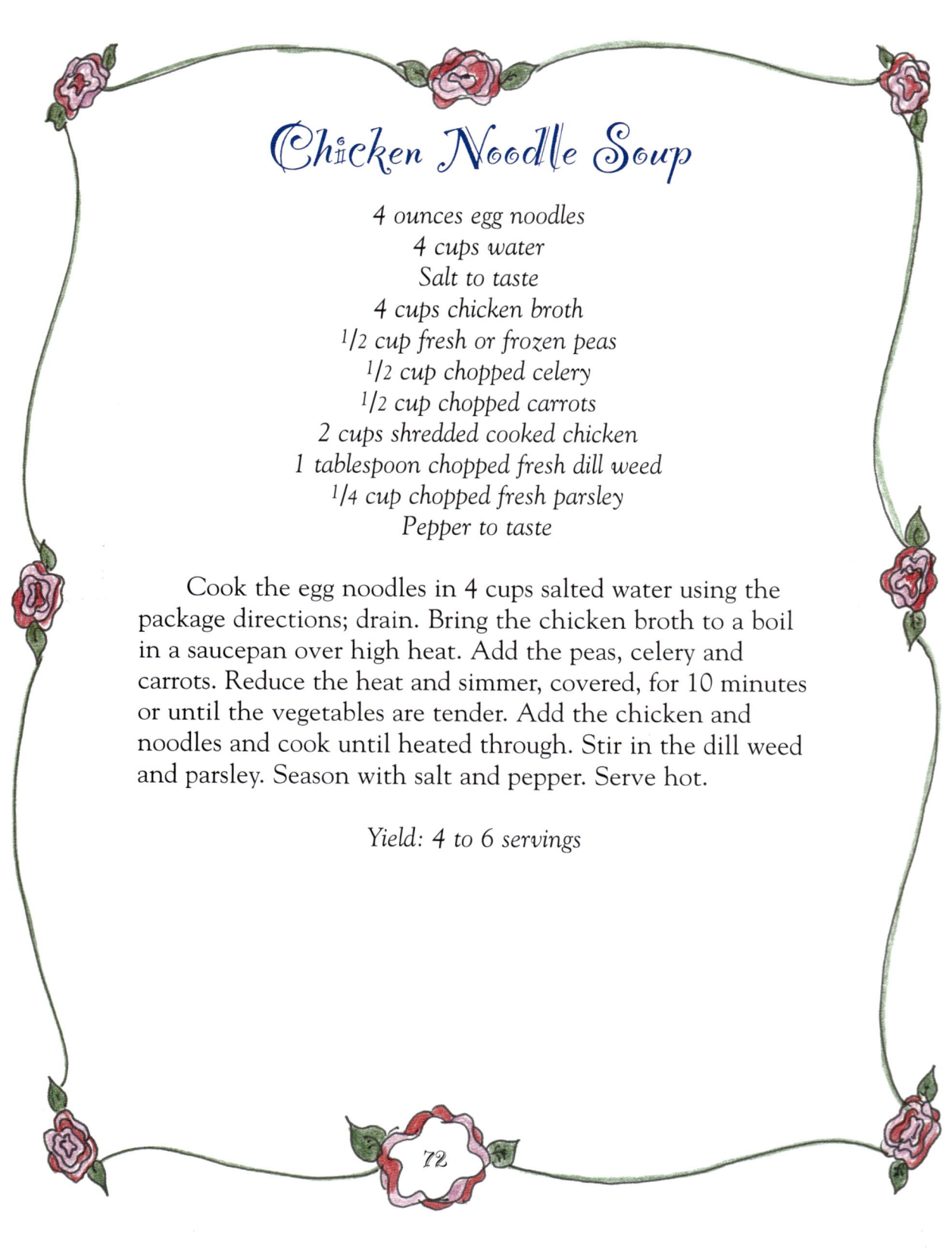

Chicken Noodle Soup

4 ounces egg noodles
4 cups water
Salt to taste
4 cups chicken broth
1/2 cup fresh or frozen peas
1/2 cup chopped celery
1/2 cup chopped carrots
2 cups shredded cooked chicken
1 tablespoon chopped fresh dill weed
1/4 cup chopped fresh parsley
Pepper to taste

Cook the egg noodles in 4 cups salted water using the package directions; drain. Bring the chicken broth to a boil in a saucepan over high heat. Add the peas, celery and carrots. Reduce the heat and simmer, covered, for 10 minutes or until the vegetables are tender. Add the chicken and noodles and cook until heated through. Stir in the dill weed and parsley. Season with salt and pepper. Serve hot.

Yield: 4 to 6 servings

Baked Potato Soup

4 large baking potatoes
2/3 cup margarine
2/3 cup flour
6 cups milk
3/4 teaspoon salt
1/2 teaspoon pepper
12 slices bacon, cooked and crumbled
1 1/2 cups (6 ounces) shredded Cheddar cheese
4 green onions, chopped (optional)
8 ounces sour cream (optional)

Bake the potatoes at 400 degrees for 1 hour. Let stand until cool. Cut the potatoes into halves lengthwise. Scoop the pulp into a bowl and discard the potato skins. Melt the margarine in a saucepan over low heat. Add the flour gradually, stirring constantly until smooth. Cook for 1 minute. Add the milk gradually, stirring constantly. Cook over medium heat until the mixture is thick and bubbly, stirring constantly. Add the potato pulp, salt, pepper, 1/2 cup of the crumbled bacon and 1 cup of the cheese and mix well. Cook until heated through, adding additional milk if necessary to reach the desired consistency. Stir in 2 tablespoons of the green onions. Ladle into soup bowls. Sprinkle with the remaining bacon, the remaining 1/2 cup cheese and the remaining green onions. Top each serving with a dollop of sour cream.

Yield: 6 to 8 servings

Side Dishes

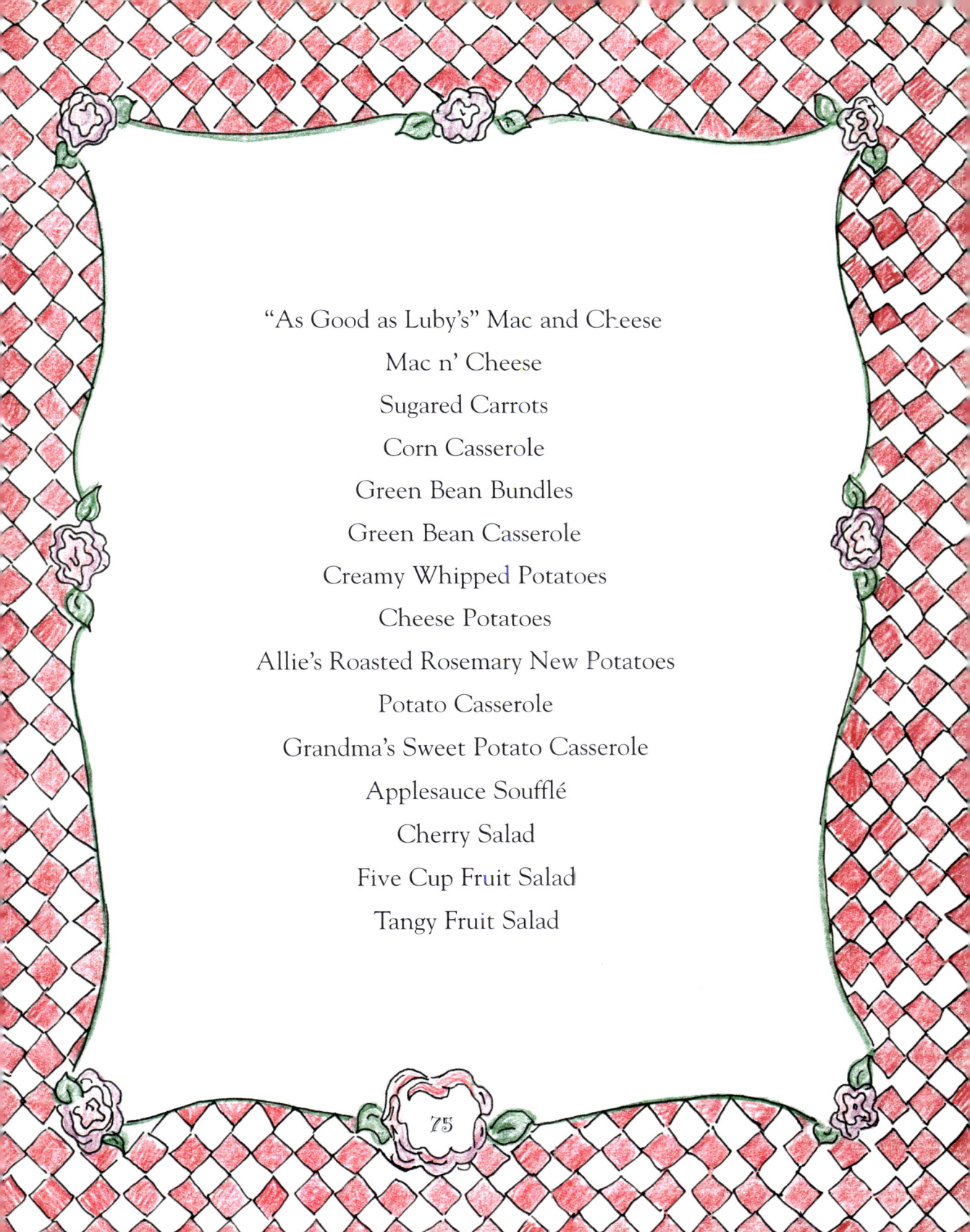

"As Good as Luby's" Mac and Cheese

Mac n' Cheese

Sugared Carrots

Corn Casserole

Green Bean Bundles

Green Bean Casserole

Creamy Whipped Potatoes

Cheese Potatoes

Allie's Roasted Rosemary New Potatoes

Potato Casserole

Grandma's Sweet Potato Casserole

Applesauce Soufflé

Cherry Salad

Five Cup Fruit Salad

Tangy Fruit Salad

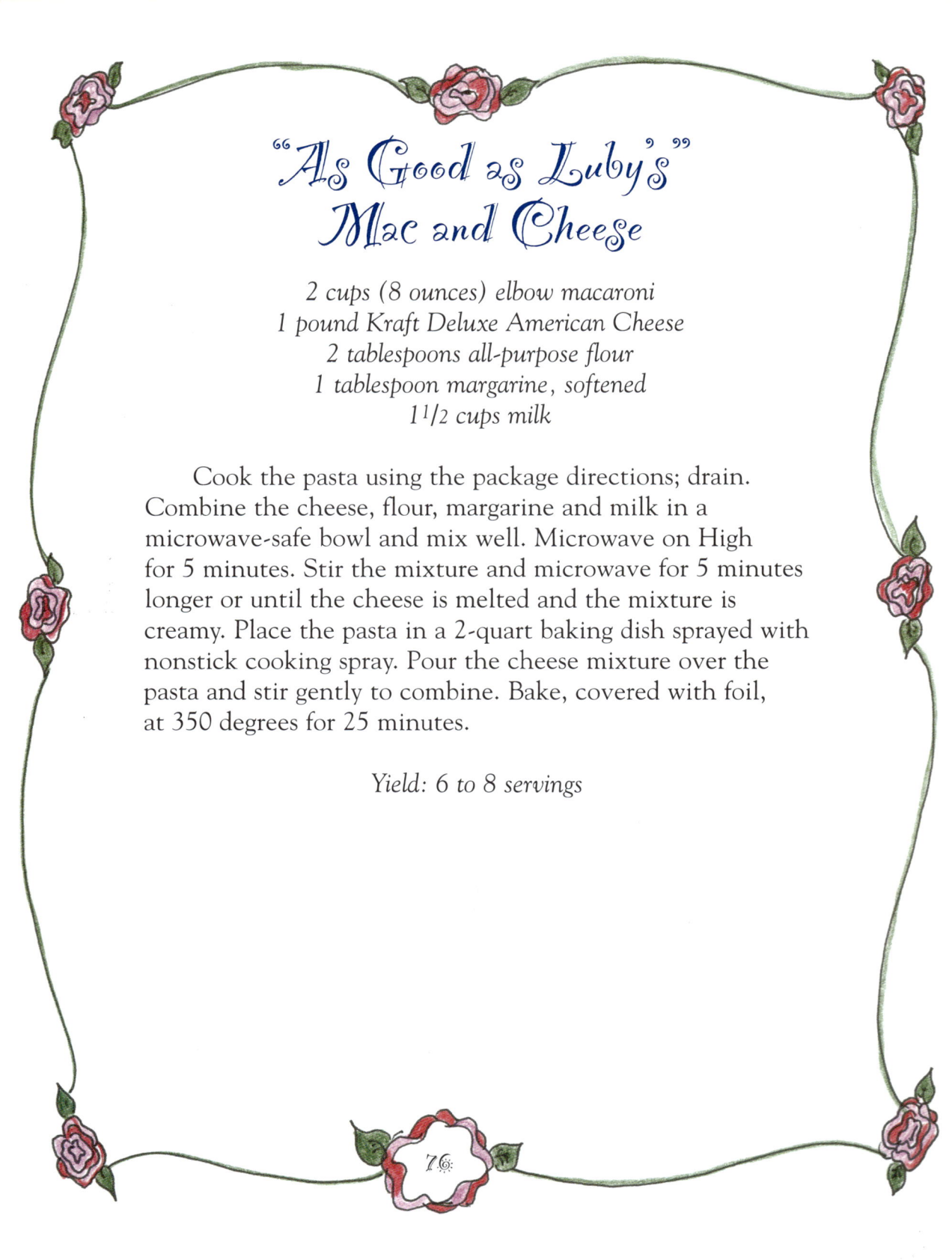

"As Good as Luby's" Mac and Cheese

2 cups (8 ounces) elbow macaroni
1 pound Kraft Deluxe American Cheese
2 tablespoons all-purpose flour
1 tablespoon margarine, softened
1 1/2 cups milk

Cook the pasta using the package directions; drain. Combine the cheese, flour, margarine and milk in a microwave-safe bowl and mix well. Microwave on High for 5 minutes. Stir the mixture and microwave for 5 minutes longer or until the cheese is melted and the mixture is creamy. Place the pasta in a 2-quart baking dish sprayed with nonstick cooking spray. Pour the cheese mixture over the pasta and stir gently to combine. Bake, covered with foil, at 350 degrees for 25 minutes.

Yield: 6 to 8 servings

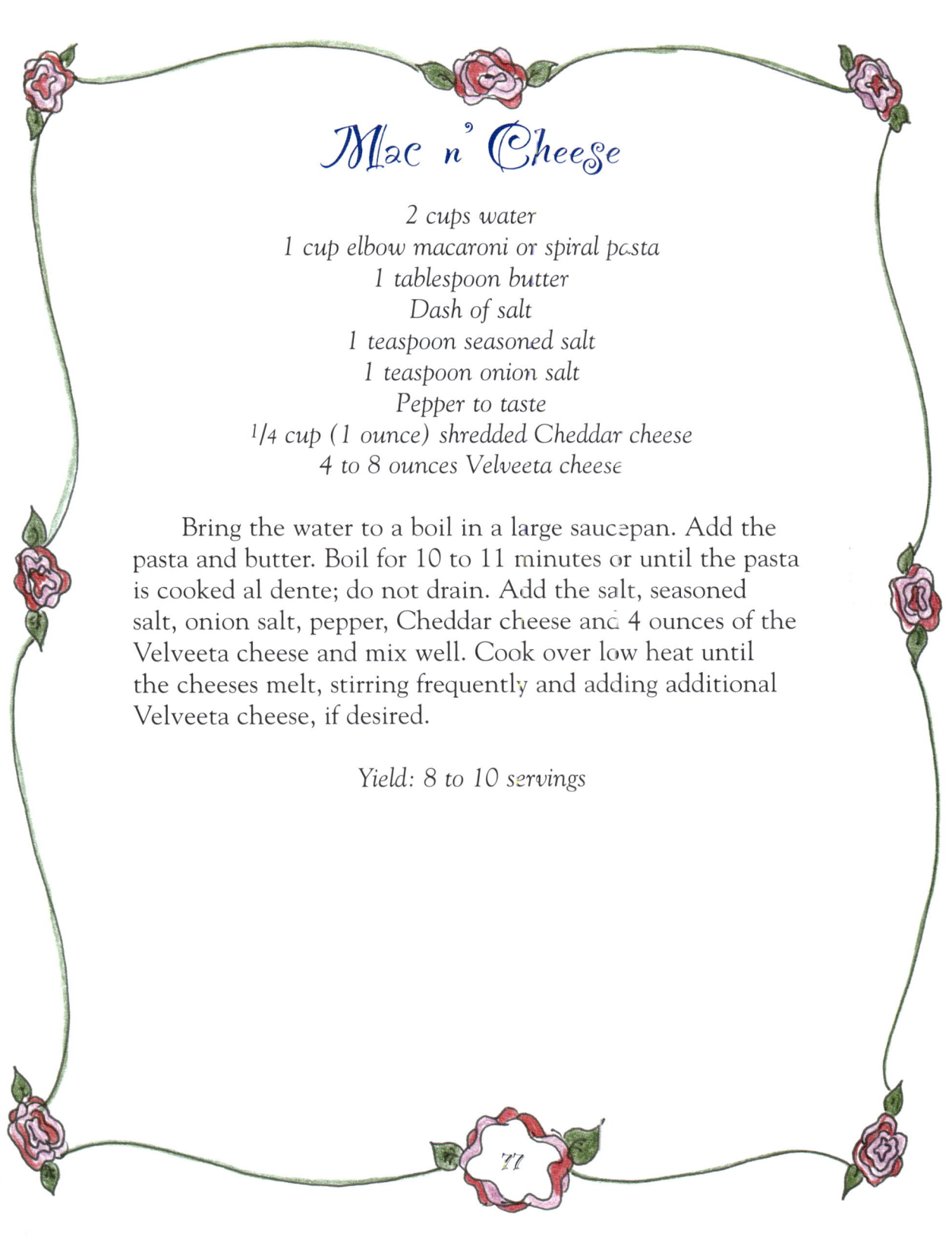

Mac n' Cheese

2 cups water
1 cup elbow macaroni or spiral pasta
1 tablespoon butter
Dash of salt
1 teaspoon seasoned salt
1 teaspoon onion salt
Pepper to taste
1/4 cup (1 ounce) shredded Cheddar cheese
4 to 8 ounces Velveeta cheese

Bring the water to a boil in a large saucepan. Add the pasta and butter. Boil for 10 to 11 minutes or until the pasta is cooked al dente; do not drain. Add the salt, seasoned salt, onion salt, pepper, Cheddar cheese and 4 ounces of the Velveeta cheese and mix well. Cook over low heat until the cheeses melt, stirring frequently and adding additional Velveeta cheese, if desired.

Yield: 8 to 10 servings

Knives

You should place your knife softly on the edge of your plate when you are not using it. Never put a knife in your mouth. The butter knife should stay with the butter dish. Don't use your own knife—which has crumbs or grease on it—to cut a piece of butter. The reason for this is the butter is for everyone to use, so you shouldn't smear it with crumbs or grease that other people then have to eat.

Sugared Carrots

2 pounds carrots, peeled and sliced
Salt to taste
1/4 cup (1/2 stick) butter, melted
1/3 cup packed brown sugar
1/3 cup granulated sugar
1/4 cup orange juice
1 teaspoon ground cinnamon
1 teaspoon vanilla extract

Cook the carrots in boiling salted water to cover in a saucepan for 5 to 10 minutes or until tender; drain. Combine the butter, brown sugar, granulated sugar, orange juice, cinnamon and vanilla in a small bowl and mix well. Spoon the carrots into a 9×9-inch glass baking dish. Pour the butter mixture over the carrots. Bake at 350 degrees for 15 to 20 minutes or until the mixture is heated through and bubbly.

Yield: 10 servings

Corn Casserole

1 (15-ounce) can cream-style corn
1 (15-ounce) can sweet corn, drained
1 (9-ounce) package Jiffy Corn Muffin Mix
1 cup sour cream
3 to 4 jalapeño chiles, finely chopped (optional)
1/2 cup (2 ounces) shredded
Cheddar cheese (optional)
Salt and pepper to taste

Mix the cream-style corn, sweet corn, corn muffin mix and sour cream in a bowl. Stir in the jalapeños and cheese. Season with salt and pepper. Spoon into a greased 9×13-inch baking dish. Bake at 350 degrees for 20 to 30 minutes.

Yield: 15 servings

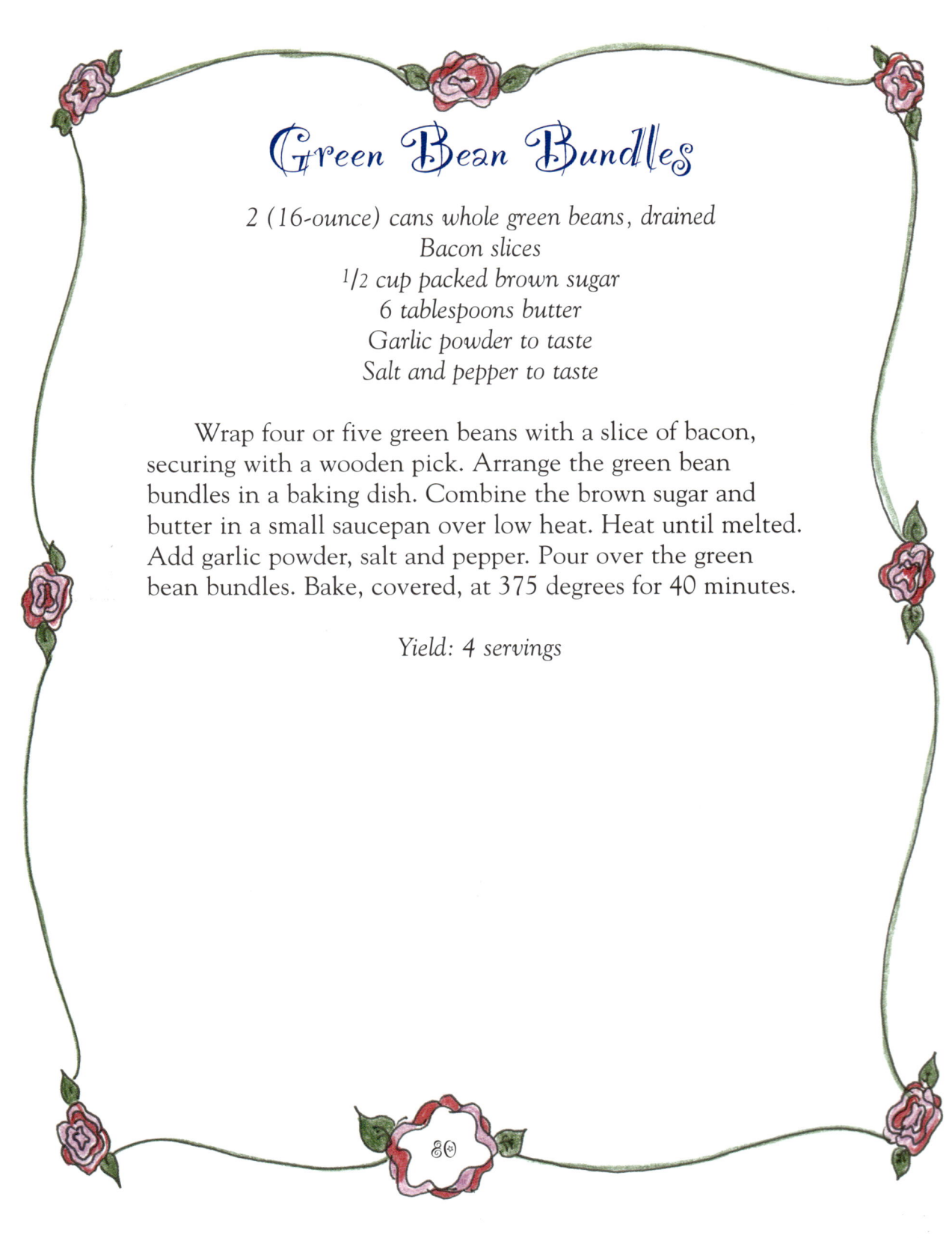

Green Bean Bundles

2 (16-ounce) cans whole green beans, drained
Bacon slices
1/2 cup packed brown sugar
6 tablespoons butter
Garlic powder to taste
Salt and pepper to taste

Wrap four or five green beans with a slice of bacon, securing with a wooden pick. Arrange the green bean bundles in a baking dish. Combine the brown sugar and butter in a small saucepan over low heat. Heat until melted. Add garlic powder, salt and pepper. Pour over the green bean bundles. Bake, covered, at 375 degrees for 40 minutes.

Yield: 4 servings

Green Bean Casserole

1/2 cup (1 stick) butter
4 ounces Velveeta cheese, cubed
1 (10-ounce) can cream of celery soup
3 to 4 (16-ounce) cans green beans, drained
1 cup croutons

Melt the butter and cheese in a skillet over medium heat, stirring frequently. Add the soup and stir until blended. Add the green beans and croutons and mix well. Spoon into a baking dish. Top with additional croutons, if desired. Bake at 350 degrees until heated through and bubbly around the edges.

Yield: 10 to 12 servings

Long Pasta

Long pasta, like spaghetti and fettuccini, should be rolled a few strands at a time onto your fork with the help of a large spoon or the side of your dish. Trailing ends of long pasta should be bitten off and returned to your plate with your fork. Do not slurp them into your mouth! Shorter pasta can easily be eaten with a fork.

Creamy Whipped Potatoes

5 large potatoes, peeled and finely chopped
(about 7^1/$_2$ cups)
2 (14-ounce) cans chicken broth
^{1}/$_2$ cup light cream or milk
^{1}/$_4$ cup (^{1}/$_2$ stick) butter or margarine
^{3}/$_4$ teaspoon salt
^{1}/$_4$ teaspoon pepper

Combine the potatoes and broth in a large saucepan and bring to a boil. Reduce the heat to medium and cook, covered, for 10 minutes or until the potatoes are tender; drain. Whip the potatoes with an electric mixer. Add the cream, butter, salt and pepper and beat until smooth. Serve immediately.

Yield: 6 servings

Cheese Potatoes

6 to 8 potatoes, peeled and chopped
1/4 cup vegetable oil
3 to 4 tablespoons all-purpose flour
2 cups 2% or whole milk
1 1/2 teaspoons garlic salt
1 1/2 teaspoons onion salt
1/2 to 3/4 teaspoon parsley
Salt and pepper to taste
1 cup (4 ounces) shredded
Colby/Cheddar cheese mix
12 ounces Velveeta cheese

Cook the potatoes in boiling water to cover in a saucepan until tender; drain. Place the potatoes in a serving dish. Combine the oil and flour in a 4-quart saucepan over medium-low heat and stir until of a paste consistency, adding additional flour if necessary. Add the milk, garlic salt, onion salt, parsley and salt and pepper and cook over medium-low heat until thickened, stirring constantly. Add the cheeses and stir until melted and the mixture is blended. Pour over the potatoes and mix gently. Serve immediately.

Yield: 12 to 15 servings

Allie's Roasted Rosemary New Potatoes

5 sprigs fresh rosemary
1/4 cup extra-virgin olive oil
8 garlic cloves, finely minced
Sea salt to taste
Freshly ground pepper to taste
1 pound red new potatoes, quartered
1 pound white new potatoes, quartered

Hold each rosemary sprig upright. Remove the leaves by running each sprig between the thumb and index finger from top to bottom. Chop the rosemary leaves. Combine the rosemary leaves and olive oil in a bowl and mix well. Add the garlic, salt and pepper and mix well. Add the potatoes and mix gently to coat. Place the potatoes in a nonstick baking dish, using a slotted spoon. Roast, covered with foil, at 375 degrees for 45 minutes.

Yield: 6 to 8 servings

Potato Casserole

12 red potatoes
1/2 cup (1 stick) butter
1 1/2 cups half-and-half
1 tablespoon salt
3 cups (12 ounces) shredded Cheddar cheese

Boil the potatoes in water to cover in a saucepan until tender; drain. Chill, covered, for 8 hours. Peel and grate the cold potatoes into a bowl. Combine the butter, half-and-half and salt in a large saucepan. Heat until the butter is melted, stirring occasionally. Add the potatoes and 2 cups of the cheese and mix well. Spoon into a baking dish. Bake at 350 degrees for 45 minutes. Sprinkle with the remaining 1 cup cheese. Bake for 15 minutes longer.

Yield: 10 servings

Meat

All meat, fish, and chicken should be cut and eaten one bite at a time so that it stays warm and juicy. You should never cut up an entire piece of meat before you begin eating. Don't stab your meat with your fork or "saw" it with your knife. Use your pointer fingers to press down so that your knife and fork cut easily through the meat. Remember to keep those elbows to your sides while you cut your food. When you are dining informally (on a picnic or at a barbecue), chicken on the bone may be eaten with your fingers.

Grandma's Sweet Potato Casserole

3 cups mashed cooked sweet potatoes
2 eggs
1/2 cup (1 stick) butter, melted
1/2 cup evaporated milk
1 teaspoon vanilla extract
3/4 cup granulated sugar
1 cup packed brown sugar
1/2 cup (1 stick) butter, melted
1/3 cup all-purpose flour
1 cup chopped pecans

Combine the sweet potatoes, eggs, 1/2 cup butter, the evaporated milk, vanilla and granulated sugar in a bowl and mix well. Spoon into a greased 9×9-inch greased glass baking dish. Combine the brown sugar, 1/2 cup butter, the flour and pecans in a bowl and mix until crumbly. Sprinkle over the sweet potato mixture. Bake at 350 degrees for 30 minutes.

Yield: 4 to 6 servings

Applesauce Soufflé

2 eggs, beaten
1/4 cup (1/2 stick) butter, melted
3/4 cup sugar
1 cup crushed vanilla wafers
1 cup milk
2 cups applesauce

Combine the eggs, butter, sugar, crushed vanilla wafers and milk in a bowl and beat until blended. Stir in the applesauce. Pour into a greased baking dish. Bake at 350 degrees for 35 to 40 minutes. You may double the recipe to feed a larger crowd.

Yield: 4 to 6 servings

Cherry Salad

1 (21-ounce) can crushed pineapple, drained
1 (21-ounce) can cherry pie filling
1 (14-ounce) can sweetened condensed milk
1/2 to 1 cup chopped nuts
16 ounces whipped topping

Combine the pineapple, cherry pie filling, sweetened condensed milk and nuts in a bowl and mix well. Fold in the whipped topping. Spoon into a serving dish. Chill, covered, until ready to serve.

Yield: 8 servings

Five-Cup Fruit Salad

1 cup pineapple chunks
1 cup mandarin oranges
1 cup frozen shredded coconut
1 cup miniature marshmallows
1 cup sour cream

Combine the pineapple, mandarin oranges, coconut, marshmallows and sour cream in a bowl and mix gently. Chill, covered, for several hours to overnight before serving.

Yield: 4 to 6 servings

Tangy Fruit Salad

1 cup sugar
2 tablespoons all-purpose flour
Juice of 2 lemons
1/2 cup pineapple juice
3 bananas, sliced
3 apples, chopped
1 (29-ounce) can pineapple tidbits, drained
1 (11-ounce) can mandarin oranges, drained
1 cup chopped pecans (optional)

Combine the sugar and flour in a saucepan. Add the lemon juice and pineapple juice and mix well. Bring the mixture to a boil, stirring constantly. Boil for 1 minute or until the mixture is thickened, stirring constantly. Pour the mixture into a bowl and chill, covered, in the refrigerator. Add the bananas, apples, pineapple, mandarin oranges and pecans to the chilled juice mixture and mix well. Serve immediately.

Yield: 10 servings

Desserts

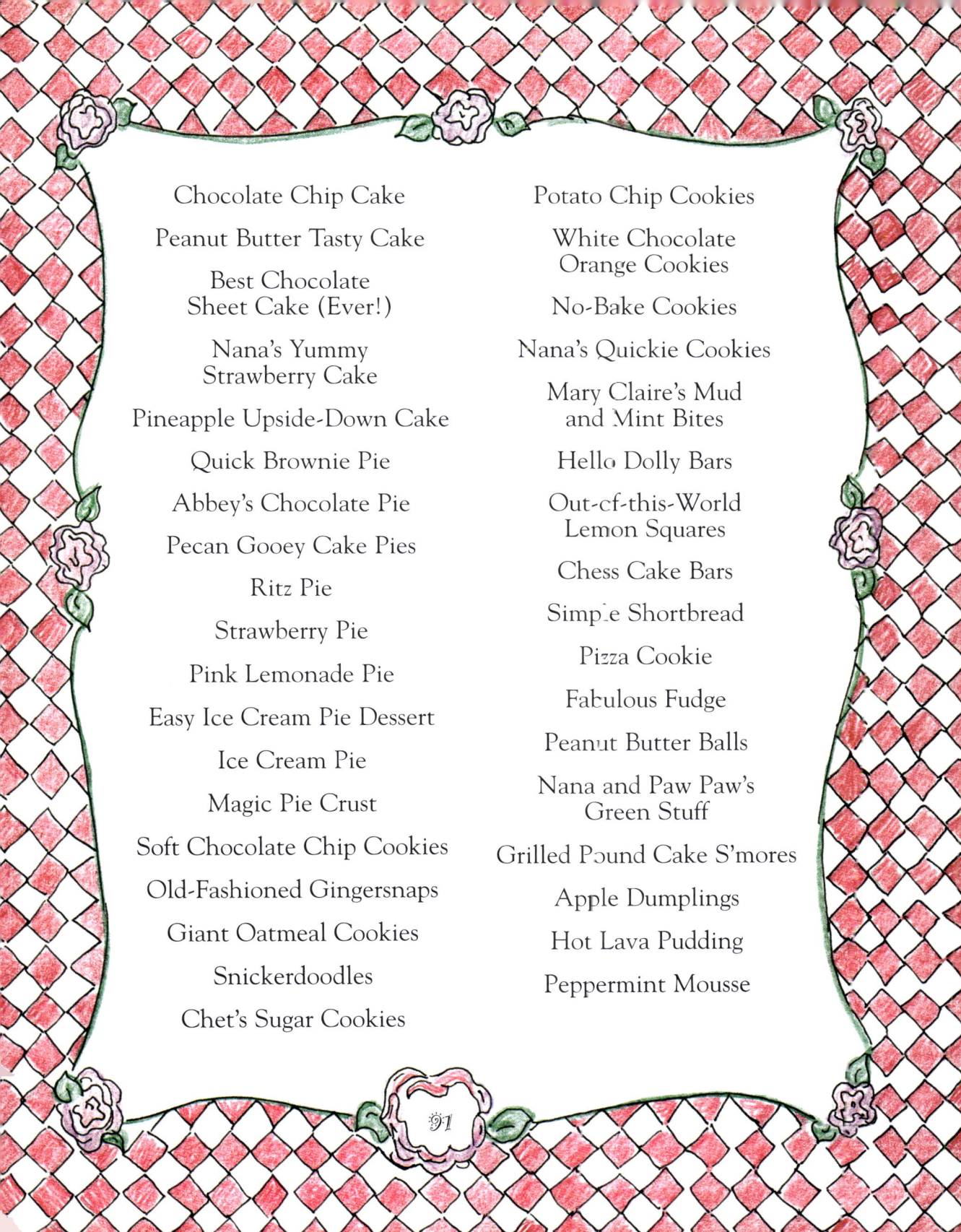

Chocolate Chip Cake

Peanut Butter Tasty Cake

Best Chocolate
Sheet Cake (Ever!)

Nana's Yummy
Strawberry Cake

Pineapple Upside-Down Cake

Quick Brownie Pie

Abbey's Chocolate Pie

Pecan Gooey Cake Pies

Ritz Pie

Strawberry Pie

Pink Lemonade Pie

Easy Ice Cream Pie Dessert

Ice Cream Pie

Magic Pie Crust

Soft Chocolate Chip Cookies

Old-Fashioned Gingersnaps

Giant Oatmeal Cookies

Snickerdoodles

Chet's Sugar Cookies

Potato Chip Cookies

White Chocolate
Orange Cookies

No-Bake Cookies

Nana's Quickie Cookies

Mary Claire's Mud
and Mint Bites

Hello Dolly Bars

Out-of-this-World
Lemon Squares

Chess Cake Bars

Simple Shortbread

Pizza Cookie

Fabulous Fudge

Peanut Butter Balls

Nana and Paw Paw's
Green Stuff

Grilled Pound Cake S'mores

Apple Dumplings

Hot Lava Pudding

Peppermint Mousse

Chocolate Chip Cake

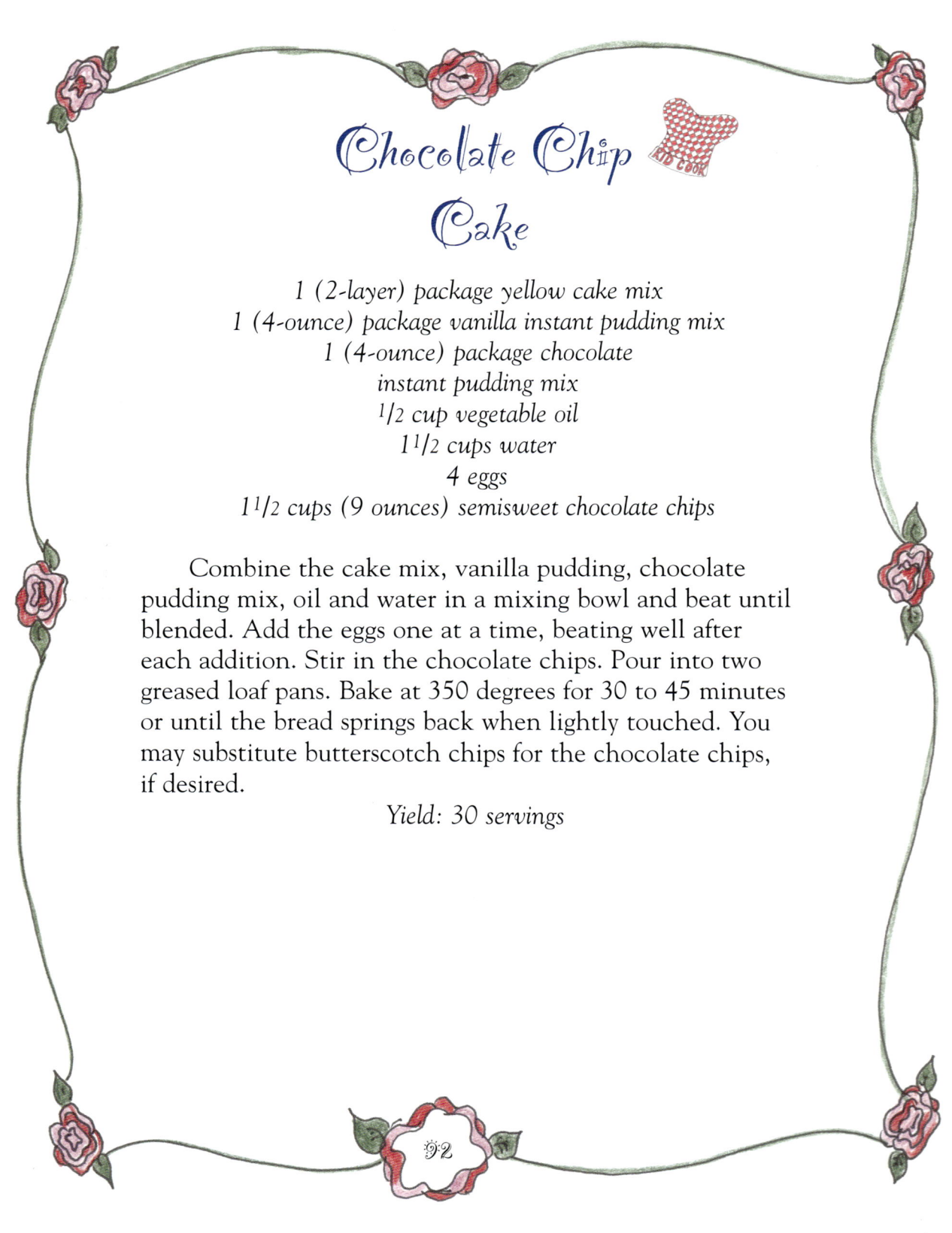

1 (2-layer) package yellow cake mix
1 (4-ounce) package vanilla instant pudding mix
1 (4-ounce) package chocolate
instant pudding mix
1/2 cup vegetable oil
1 1/2 cups water
4 eggs
1 1/2 cups (9 ounces) semisweet chocolate chips

Combine the cake mix, vanilla pudding, chocolate pudding mix, oil and water in a mixing bowl and beat until blended. Add the eggs one at a time, beating well after each addition. Stir in the chocolate chips. Pour into two greased loaf pans. Bake at 350 degrees for 30 to 45 minutes or until the bread springs back when lightly touched. You may substitute butterscotch chips for the chocolate chips, if desired.

Yield: 30 servings

Peanut Butter Tasty Cake

1 cup milk
2 teaspoons margarine
4 eggs
1 teaspoon vanilla extract
2 cups sugar
2 cups all-purpose flour
2 teaspoons baking powder
2 cups peanut butter
2 cups (12 ounces) milk chocolate chips

Combine the milk and margarine in a small saucepan. Heat until bubbles begin to form around the edge of the pan. Do not boil. Combine the eggs, vanilla and sugar in a mixing bowl and beat until blended. Add the flour and baking powder and mix well. Stir in the milk mixture. Pour into a greased and floured 10×15-inch baking pan. Bake at 350 degrees for 20 minutes or until the cake springs back when lightly touched. Spread the peanut butter over the hot cake. Chill in the refrigerator or freezer until the peanut butter hardens. Melt the chocolate chips in a small saucepan over low heat. Spread over the peanut butter. Cut into squares while the chocolate is still warm.

Yield: 16 servings

Napkin

When you sit down at the table, the first thing you do is open your napkin halfway and put it in your lap. If you must leave the table during a meal, place your napkin on your chair. Never put your used napkin on the table during a meal. When you are done eating, pick up your napkin loosely and place it on the table to the right of your plate.

Best Chocolate Sheet Cake (Ever!)

2 cups all-purpose flour
2 cups sugar
1/2 teaspoon salt
1/2 cup (1 stick) butter (no substitutions)
1 cup water
1/2 cup vegetable oil
3 tablespoons baking cocoa
1 teaspoon baking soda
1/2 cup buttermilk
2 eggs
2 teaspoons Mexican vanilla extract
Chocolate Icing (page 95)

Combine the flour, sugar and salt in a bowl. Melt the butter in a saucepan over medium heat. Stir in the water, oil and baking cocoa. Pour over the flour mixture and mix well. Combine the baking soda and buttermilk in a small bowl and stir until blended. Stir into the chocolate mixture. Combine the eggs and vanilla in a small mixing bowl and beat until blended. Pour into the chocolate mixture and mix well. Pour into a lightly greased 10×15-inch baking pan. Bake at 350 degrees for 20 minutes. Pour the Chocolate Icing over the hot cake.

Yield: 16 servings

Chocolate Icing

1/2 cup (1 stick) butter
6 tablespoons milk
3 tablespoons baking cocoa
4 cups confectioners' sugar
2 teaspoons Mexican vanilla extract
1 cup chopped nuts (optional)

Combine the butter, milk and baking cocoa in a saucepan. Heat over medium heat until the butter melts, stirring frequently. Remove from the heat and whisk in the confectioners' sugar. Stir in the vanilla and nuts.

Yield: about 5 cups

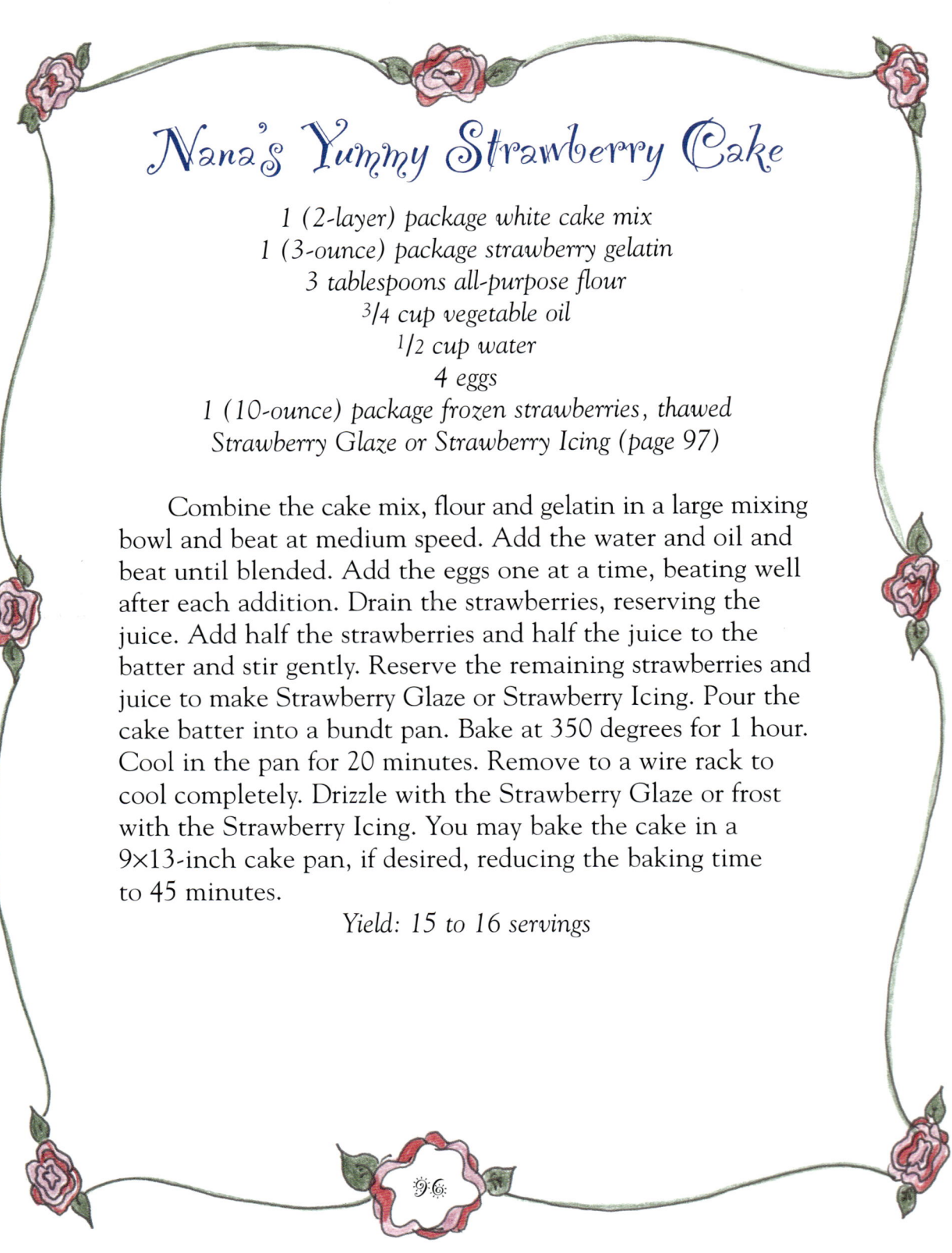

Nana's Yummy Strawberry Cake

1 (2-layer) package white cake mix
1 (3-ounce) package strawberry gelatin
3 tablespoons all-purpose flour
3/4 cup vegetable oil
1/2 cup water
4 eggs
1 (10-ounce) package frozen strawberries, thawed
Strawberry Glaze or Strawberry Icing (page 97)

Combine the cake mix, flour and gelatin in a large mixing bowl and beat at medium speed. Add the water and oil and beat until blended. Add the eggs one at a time, beating well after each addition. Drain the strawberries, reserving the juice. Add half the strawberries and half the juice to the batter and stir gently. Reserve the remaining strawberries and juice to make Strawberry Glaze or Strawberry Icing. Pour the cake batter into a bundt pan. Bake at 350 degrees for 1 hour. Cool in the pan for 20 minutes. Remove to a wire rack to cool completely. Drizzle with the Strawberry Glaze or frost with the Strawberry Icing. You may bake the cake in a 9×13-inch cake pan, if desired, reducing the baking time to 45 minutes.

Yield: 15 to 16 servings

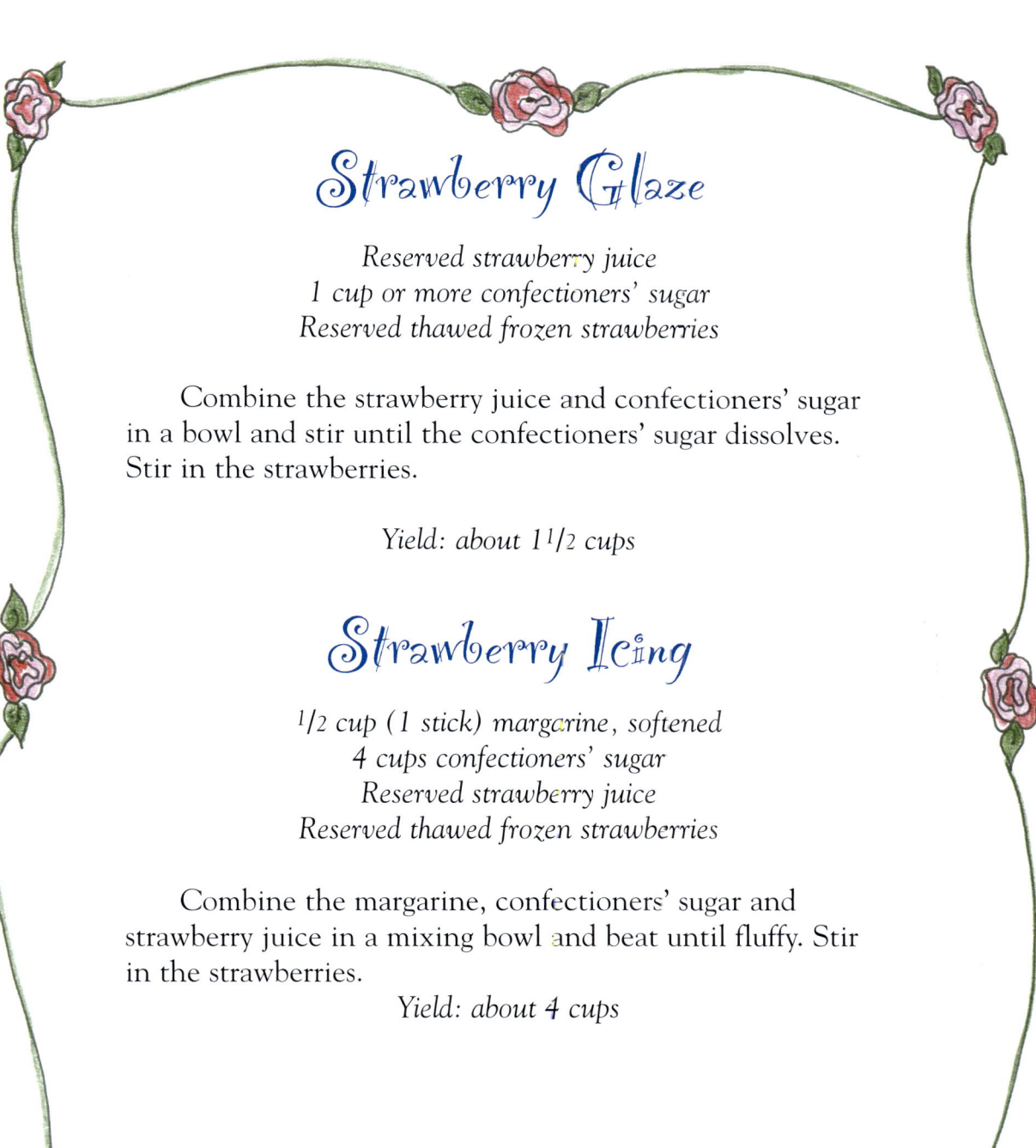

Strawberry Glaze

Reserved strawberry juice
1 cup or more confectioners' sugar
Reserved thawed frozen strawberries

Combine the strawberry juice and confectioners' sugar in a bowl and stir until the confectioners' sugar dissolves. Stir in the strawberries.

Yield: about 1 1/2 cups

Strawberry Icing

1/2 cup (1 stick) margarine, softened
4 cups confectioners' sugar
Reserved strawberry juice
Reserved thawed frozen strawberries

Combine the margarine, confectioners' sugar and strawberry juice in a mixing bowl and beat until fluffy. Stir in the strawberries.

Yield: about 4 cups

Pineapple Upside-Down Cakes

1/4 cup (1/2 stick) butter
2/3 cup packed brown sugar
2 (15-ounce) cans sliced pineapple, drained
Maraschino cherries
1 (2-layer) package butter-recipe cake mix
2/3 cup water
1/2 cup (1 stick) butter, softened
3 eggs

Line the bottoms of two 9-inch cake pans with waxed paper. Place 2 tablespoons of the butter in each pan. Melt the butter in a 375-degree oven. Sprinkle 1/3 cup of the brown sugar in each pan. Arrange the pineapple slices in the pans. Cut 7 to 8 cherries into halves. Place a cherry, cut side up, in the center of each pineapple slice. Combine the cake mix, water, 1/2 cup butter and the eggs in a mixing bowl and beat until blended. Pour the cake batter evenly into the prepared pans. Bake at 375 degrees for 25 to 35 minutes or until the cakes test done. Let the cakes cool in the pans for 15 minutes. Invert onto serving plates.

Yield: 8 servings per cake or 16 servings

Quick Brownie Pie

8 ounces semisweet chocolate
1/2 cup (1 stick) butter or margarine
1 cup sugar
2 eggs
1 teaspoon vanilla extract
1 cup all-purpose flour

Combine the chocolate and butter in a saucepan. Cook over medium heat until the butter and chocolate are melted, stirring frequently. Remove from the heat and stir in the sugar. Pour into a mixing bowl. Add the eggs and beat until blended. Stir in the vanilla. Add the flour and mix well. Pour into a buttered pie plate. Bake at 325 degrees for 25 minutes. The pie will be soft in the center. Serve with whipped cream or ice cream.

Yield: 8 servings

Offer Thanks

Giving thanks or saying grace is often done before a meal. If it is said, you wait to begin eating until it is completed. It is disrespectful to giggle and look around while someone is saying grace. It is nice to bless the cook who prepared the food you are about to eat.

Abbey's Chocolate Pie

1 (6-ounce) package chocolate instant pudding mix
3 cups milk
8 ounces whipped topping
1 (9-inch) graham cracker pie shell

Prepare the pudding mix with the milk using the package directions. Fold half the whipped topping into the pudding mixture. Spoon into the pie shell. Spread the remaining whipped topping over the pie. Chill for 1 hour or longer before serving.

Yield: 6 to 8 servings

Pecan Gooey Cake Pies

1 1/4 cups (2 1/2 sticks) butter, softened
2 1/2 cups sugar
4 eggs
2 tablespoons water
1/4 teaspoon vanilla extract
5 tablespoons corn syrup
2 cups cake flour
2 1/2 tablespoons ground cinnamon
2 unbaked (9-inch) pie shells
1/2 cup (or more) pecan halves or chopped pecans

Cream the butter and sugar in a mixing bowl until light and fluffy. Add the eggs one at a time, beating well after each addition. Combine the water, vanilla and corn syrup in a small bowl and mix well. Add to the creamed mixture gradually, beating constantly. Combine the flour and cinnamon in a bowl. Add to the creamed mixture gradually, beating constantly at low speed. Pour the batter evenly into the pie shells. Sprinkle evenly with the pecans. Bake at 350 degrees for 45 minutes or until dark golden brown. The pies will be soft in the center.

Yield: 16 servings

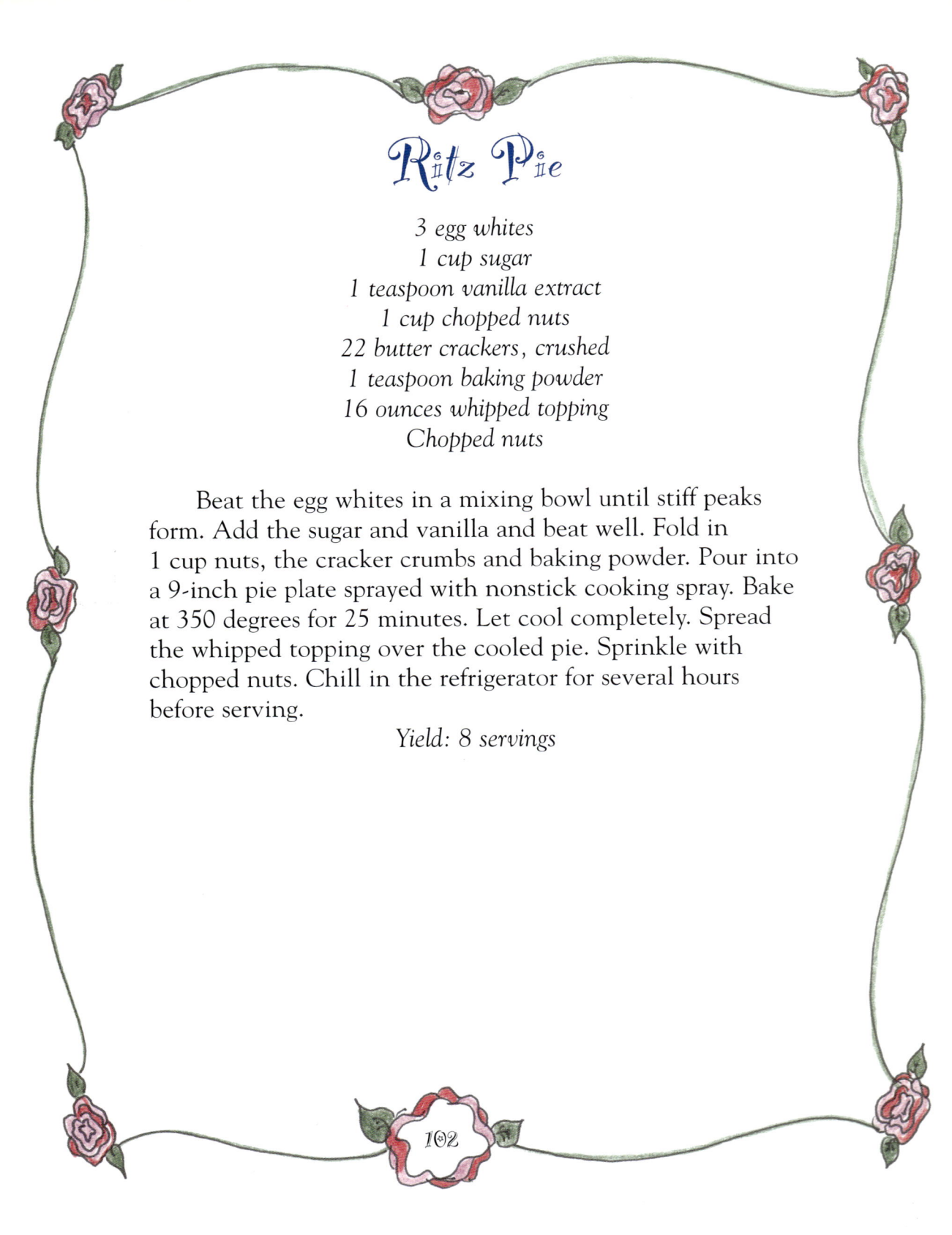

Ritz Pie

3 egg whites
1 cup sugar
1 teaspoon vanilla extract
1 cup chopped nuts
22 butter crackers, crushed
1 teaspoon baking powder
16 ounces whipped topping
Chopped nuts

Beat the egg whites in a mixing bowl until stiff peaks form. Add the sugar and vanilla and beat well. Fold in 1 cup nuts, the cracker crumbs and baking powder. Pour into a 9-inch pie plate sprayed with nonstick cooking spray. Bake at 350 degrees for 25 minutes. Let cool completely. Spread the whipped topping over the cooled pie. Sprinkle with chopped nuts. Chill in the refrigerator for several hours before serving.

Yield: 8 servings

Strawberry Pie

1 (9-inch) graham cracker pie shell
1 egg white
4 cups sliced fresh strawberries
3/4 cup sugar
2 tablespoons cornstarch
1 1/2 cups water
1 (3-ounce) package strawberry gelatin

Brush the pie shell with the egg white. Bake at
375 degrees for 5 minutes. Let stand until cool. Fill the
cooled pie shell with the strawberries. Combine the sugar,
cornstarch and water in a saucepan. Bring to a boil over
low heat, whisking constantly. Simmer for 2 minutes,
stirring frequently. Add the gelatin and mix well. Pour
over the strawberries. Chill in the refrigerator for 2 to
3 hours. Serve with whipped topping.

Yield: 8 servings

Pink Lemonade Pie

*1 (12-ounce) can frozen pink
lemonade concentrate, thawed
8 ounces whipped topping
1 (14-ounce) can sweetened condensed milk
1 (9-inch) graham cracker pie shell*

Combine the lemonade concentrate, whipped topping and sweetened condensed milk in a bowl and mix well. Pour the mixture into the pie shell. Chill in the refrigerator until ready to serve.

Yield: 8 servings

Easy Ice Cream Pie Dessert

*1 package miniature ice cream sandwiches
12 ounces whipped topping
2 Butterfinger candy bars, crushed*

Arrange a layer of the ice cream sandwiches in a 9×13-inch dish. Spread with the whipped topping. Sprinkle with the candy bar crumbs. Freeze, covered, until ready to serve.

Yield: 15 servings

Ice Cream Pie

1/4 cup corn syrup
3 tablespoons butter
2 tablespoons brown sugar
2 1/2 cups crisp rice cereal
1/4 cup peanut butter
3 tablespoons corn syrup
Chocolate syrup
1 to 1 1/2 pints vanilla ice cream, softened

Combine 1/4 cup corn syrup, the butter and brown sugar in a saucepan. Bring to a boil, stirring frequently. Remove from the heat and stir in the cereal. Press the mixture into a pie plate. Combine the peanut butter, 3 tablespoons corn syrup and a generous squeeze of chocolate syrup in a bowl and mix well. Spread over the cereal mixture. Freeze until firm. Spoon the ice cream over the peanut butter layer and freeze until firm. Drizzle with chocolate syrup before serving.

Yield: 8 servings

Magic Pie Crust

3 cups all-purpose flour
1 teaspoon salt
1 1/2 cups shortening
1 egg, slightly beaten
6 tablespoons water
1 teaspoon vinegar

Combine the flour and salt in a bowl. Cut in the shortening with two knives or a pastry blender until the mixture resembles coarse crumbs. Combine the egg and water in a bowl and mix well. Sprinkle over the flour mixture. Add the vinegar and stir gently until the mixture forms a ball. Chill, wrapped in waxed paper, until ready to use. To prepare, divide the dough into thirds. Roll out one-third of the dough on a floured surface. Line a 9-inch pie plate with the dough. Bake at 425 degrees for 10 to 12 minutes or until golden brown.

Yield: three 9-inch pie shells or two 10-inch pie shells

Soft Chocolate Chip Cookies

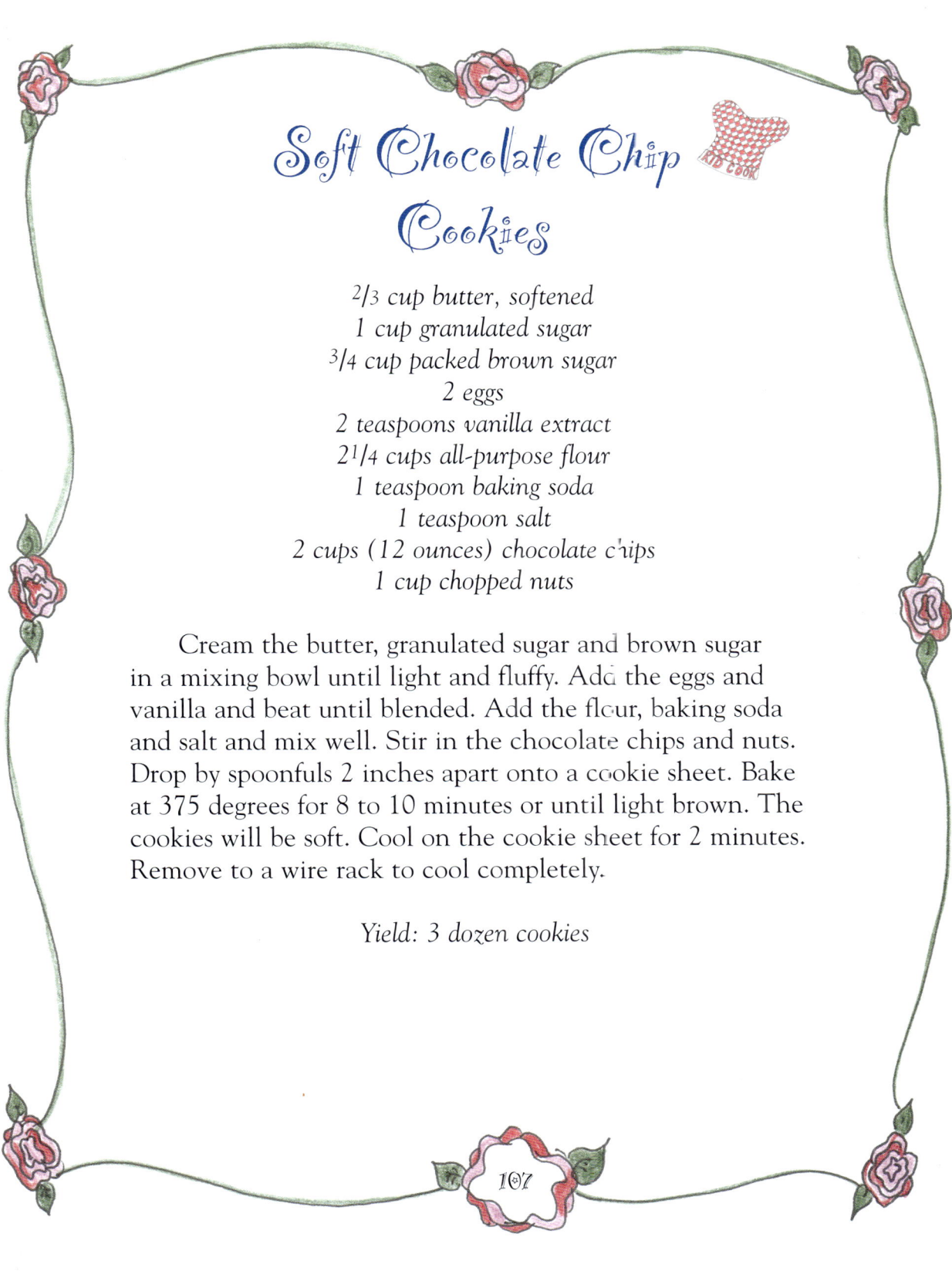

2/3 cup butter, softened
1 cup granulated sugar
3/4 cup packed brown sugar
2 eggs
2 teaspoons vanilla extract
2 1/4 cups all-purpose flour
1 teaspoon baking soda
1 teaspoon salt
2 cups (12 ounces) chocolate chips
1 cup chopped nuts

Cream the butter, granulated sugar and brown sugar in a mixing bowl until light and fluffy. Add the eggs and vanilla and beat until blended. Add the flour, baking soda and salt and mix well. Stir in the chocolate chips and nuts. Drop by spoonfuls 2 inches apart onto a cookie sheet. Bake at 375 degrees for 8 to 10 minutes or until light brown. The cookies will be soft. Cool on the cookie sheet for 2 minutes. Remove to a wire rack to cool completely.

Yield: 3 dozen cookies

Passing at the Table

Pass all serving dishes to the right. When you pass a dish that has a handle (cream pitcher, gravy boat), turn it so that the person to whom you are passing it can take hold of the handle. Always pass the salt and pepper shakers together.

☆Old-Fashioned Gingersnaps

2 cups all-purpose flour
2 teaspoons baking soda
1/4 teaspoon salt
1 teaspoon ground cinnamon
1/2 teaspoon ground cloves
1 teaspoon ginger
3/4 cup shortening
(do not substitute butter or margarine)
1 cup sugar
1 egg
1/4 cup molasses
Sugar

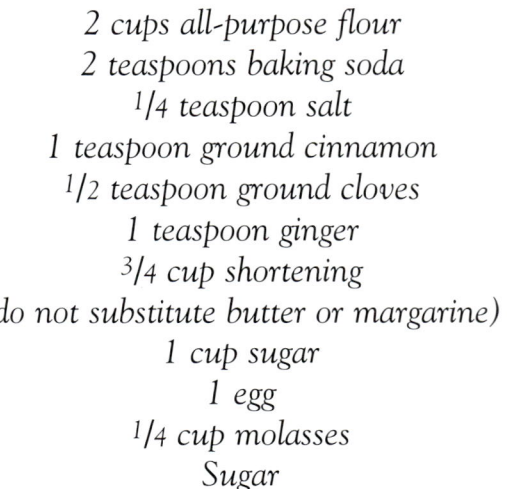

Sift the flour, baking soda, salt, cinnamon, cloves and ginger together. Cream the shortening, 1 cup sugar and the egg in a mixing bowl until light and fluffy. Add the molasses and beat until blended. Add the flour mixture and mix well. Chill, covered, for 1 hour. Shape into 1-inch balls. Roll in sugar and arrange on an ungreased cookie sheet. Bake at 375 degrees for 8 to 10 minutes or until brown. Cool for 2 minutes. Remove to a wire rack to cool completely.

Yield: 60 cookies

Giant Oatmeal Cookies

1^1/2 cups raisins
2 cups all-purpose flour
1^1/8 teaspoons salt
2^1/8 teaspoons baking powder
^{1}/2 teaspoon baking soda
1 cup shortening
^{3}/4 cup plus 2 tablespoons granulated sugar
1^1/3 cups packed brown sugar
2 eggs
2 tablespoons water
1^1/2 teaspoons vanilla extract
3^3/4 cups rolled oats

Soak the raisins in warm water to cover in a bowl for 10 minutes; drain. Sift the next four ingredients together. Cream the shortening and sugars in a mixing bowl until light and fluffy. Stir in the eggs, 2 tablespoons water and the vanilla. Beat in the flour mixture at low speed for 2 to 3 minutes or until smooth. Stir in the oats and raisins. Shape into 2-inch-thick logs. Chill, wrapped in waxed paper, until firm. Cut the logs into ^{1}/2-inch slices and place on a cookie sheet. Flatten to ^{1}/4 inch with the back of a spoon. Bake at 375 degrees for 10 to 12 minutes or until golden brown.

Yield: 3 dozen cookies

Snickerdoodles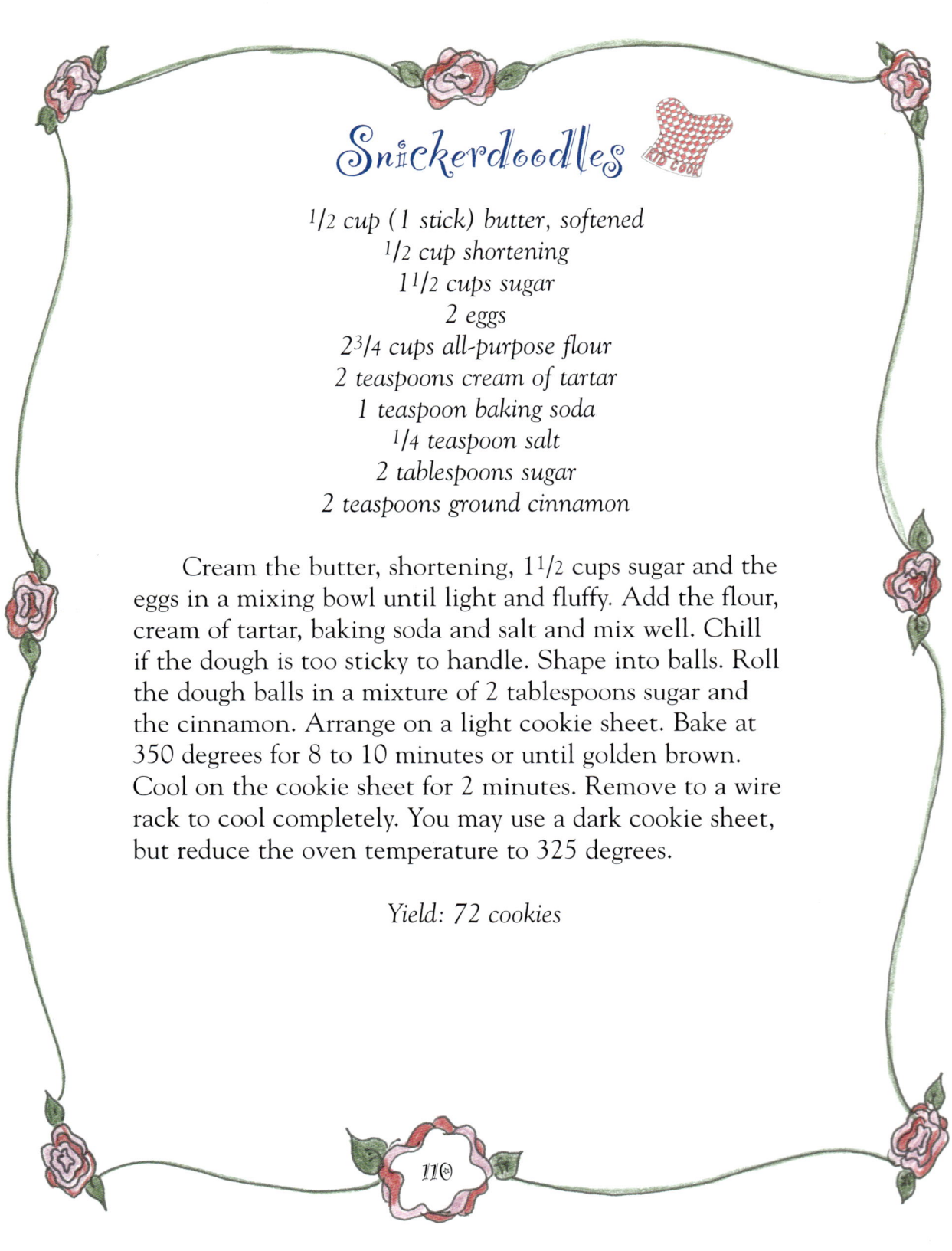

1/2 cup (1 stick) butter, softened
1/2 cup shortening
1 1/2 cups sugar
2 eggs
2 3/4 cups all-purpose flour
2 teaspoons cream of tartar
1 teaspoon baking soda
1/4 teaspoon salt
2 tablespoons sugar
2 teaspoons ground cinnamon

Cream the butter, shortening, 1 1/2 cups sugar and the eggs in a mixing bowl until light and fluffy. Add the flour, cream of tartar, baking soda and salt and mix well. Chill if the dough is too sticky to handle. Shape into balls. Roll the dough balls in a mixture of 2 tablespoons sugar and the cinnamon. Arrange on a light cookie sheet. Bake at 350 degrees for 8 to 10 minutes or until golden brown. Cool on the cookie sheet for 2 minutes. Remove to a wire rack to cool completely. You may use a dark cookie sheet, but reduce the oven temperature to 325 degrees.

Yield: 72 cookies

Chet's Sugar Cookies

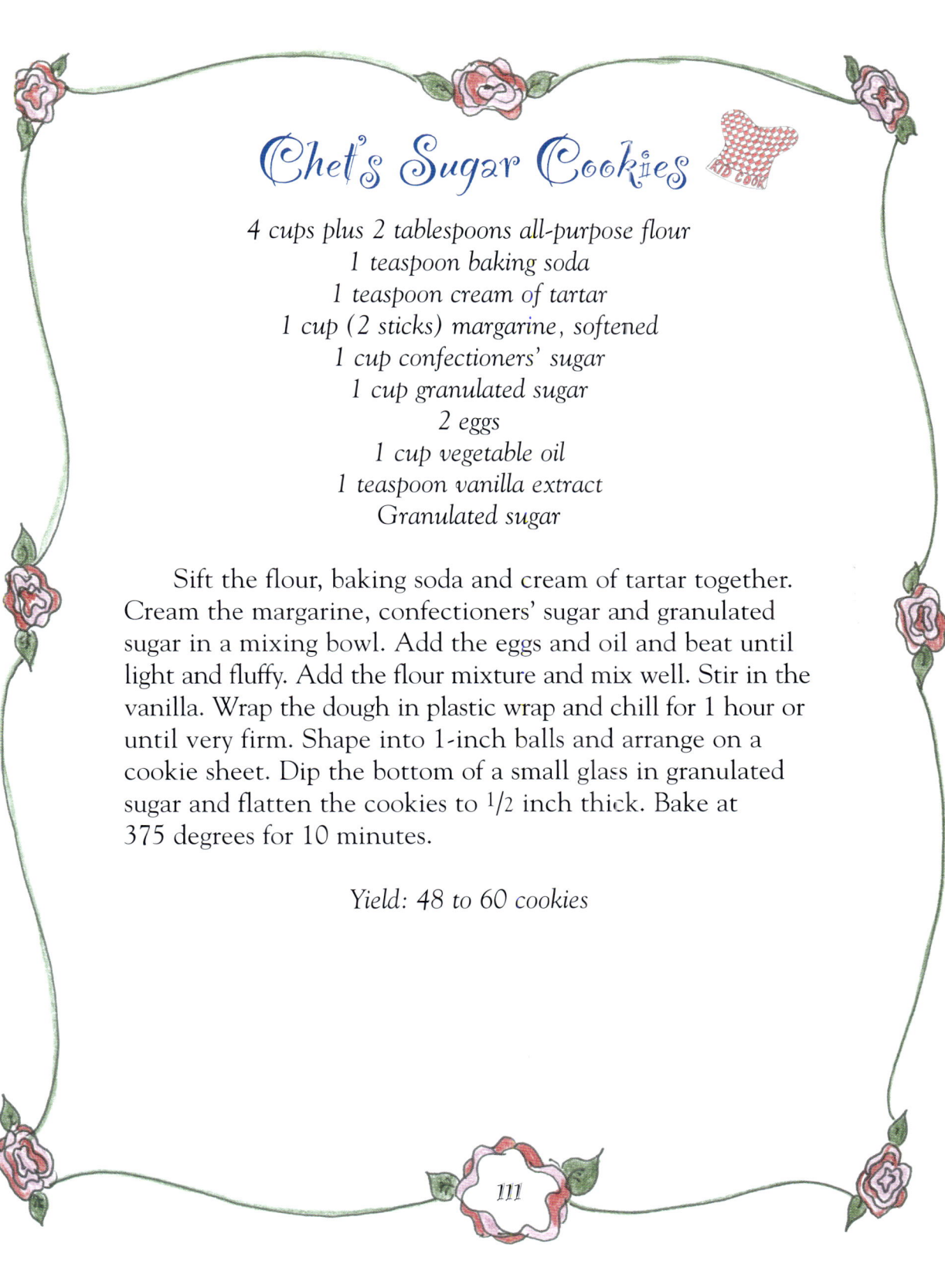

4 cups plus 2 tablespoons all-purpose flour
1 teaspoon baking soda
1 teaspoon cream of tartar
1 cup (2 sticks) margarine, softened
1 cup confectioners' sugar
1 cup granulated sugar
2 eggs
1 cup vegetable oil
1 teaspoon vanilla extract
Granulated sugar

Sift the flour, baking soda and cream of tartar together. Cream the margarine, confectioners' sugar and granulated sugar in a mixing bowl. Add the eggs and oil and beat until light and fluffy. Add the flour mixture and mix well. Stir in the vanilla. Wrap the dough in plastic wrap and chill for 1 hour or until very firm. Shape into 1-inch balls and arrange on a cookie sheet. Dip the bottom of a small glass in granulated sugar and flatten the cookies to 1/2 inch thick. Bake at 375 degrees for 10 minutes.

Yield: 48 to 60 cookies

Quietly Drink from a Straw

When you have a drink that you have placed a straw in, you should sip from the straw quietly—not slurping and making loud noises. If you will leave a little liquid at the bottom of your glass, you can avoid making a slurping sound. It is not appropriate to blow bubbles in your milk with a straw either!

Potato Chip Cookies

2 cups (4 sticks) butter, softened
1 cup granulated sugar
1 teaspoon vanilla extract
3 cups all-purpose flour
1 1/2 cups crushed Ruffles potato chips
Confectioners' sugar

Cream the butter, granulated sugar and vanilla in a large mixing bowl. Add the flour 1 cup at a time, mixing well after each addition. Stir in the potato chips. Drop by teaspoonfuls onto an ungreased cookie sheet. Bake at 350 degrees for 10 to 15 minutes or until golden brown. Cool on the cookie sheet for 2 minutes. Remove to a wire rack to cool completely. Sprinkle with confectioners' sugar.

Yield: 4 dozen cookies

White Chocolate Orange Cookies

2 1/4 cups all-purpose flour
3/4 teaspoon baking soda
1/2 teaspoon salt
1 cup (2 sticks) butter or margarine, softened
2/3 cup packed brown sugar
1/2 cup granulated sugar
1 egg
2 tablespoons orange extract
1 tablespoon grated orange zest
2 cups (12 ounces) white chocolate chips

Combine the flour, baking soda and salt in a bowl. Cream the butter, brown sugar and granulated sugar in a mixing bowl until light and fluffy. Add the egg, orange extract and orange zest and beat until blended. Add the flour mixture gradually, beating just until blended after each addition. Stir in the white chocolate chips. Drop by rounded tablespoonfuls onto a greased cookie sheet. Bake at 350 degrees for 10 to 12 minutes or until the edges are light brown. Cool on the cookie sheet for 2 minutes. Remove to a wire rack to cool completely.

Yield: 42 cookies

No-Bake Cookies

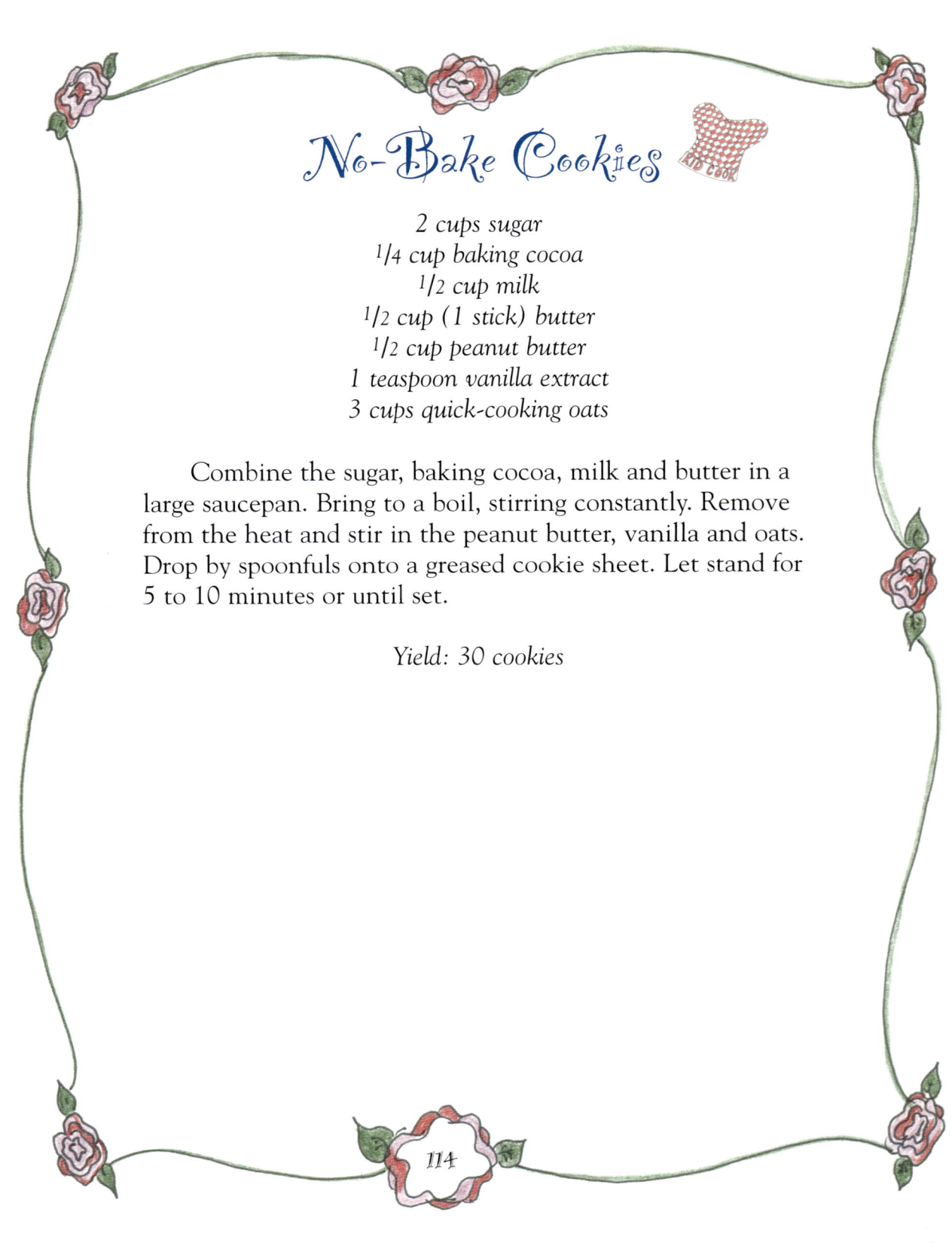

2 cups sugar
1/4 cup baking cocoa
1/2 cup milk
1/2 cup (1 stick) butter
1/2 cup peanut butter
1 teaspoon vanilla extract
3 cups quick-cooking oats

Combine the sugar, baking cocoa, milk and butter in a large saucepan. Bring to a boil, stirring constantly. Remove from the heat and stir in the peanut butter, vanilla and oats. Drop by spoonfuls onto a greased cookie sheet. Let stand for 5 to 10 minutes or until set.

Yield: 30 cookies

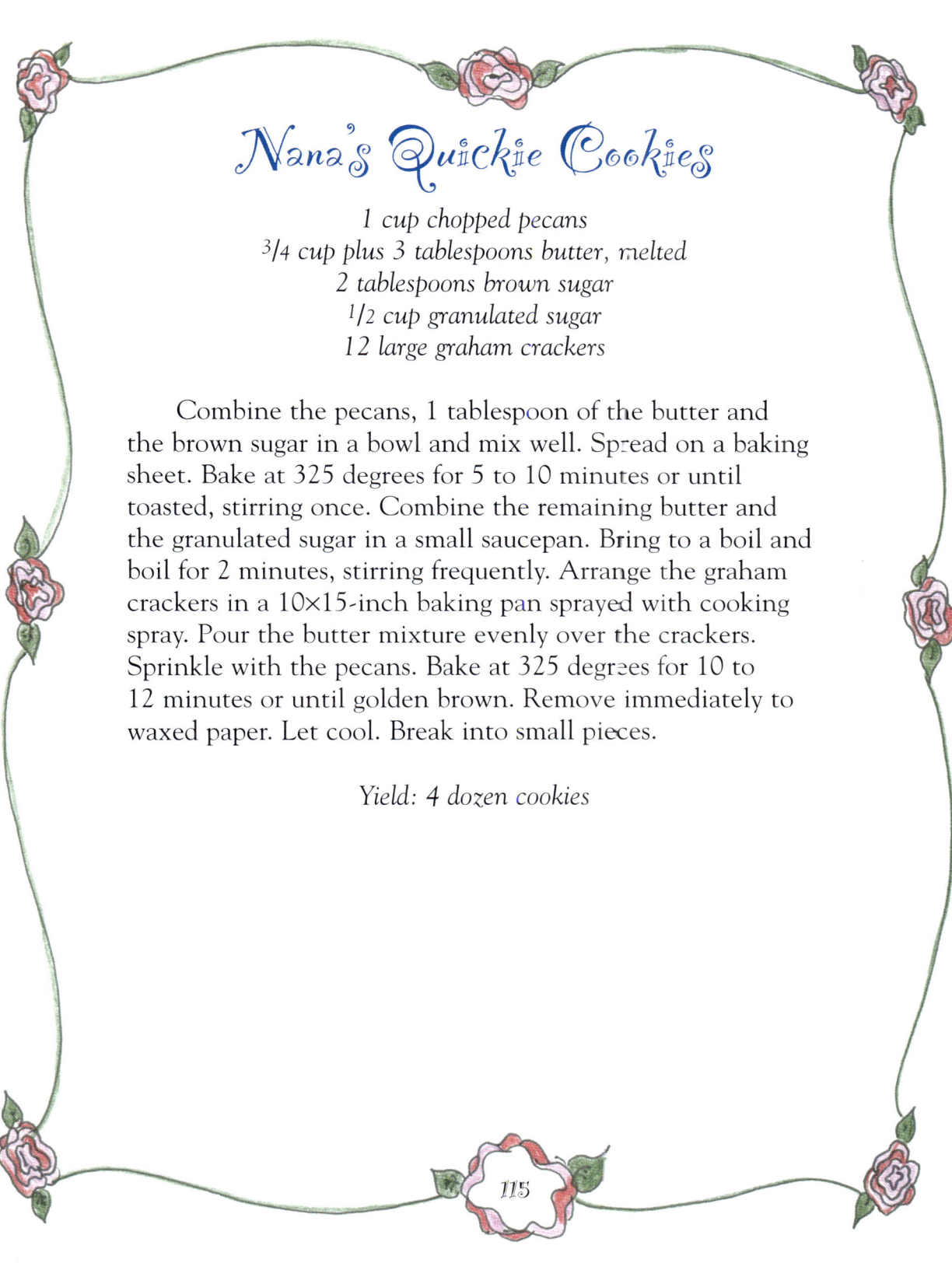

Nana's Quickie Cookies

1 cup chopped pecans
3/4 cup plus 3 tablespoons butter, melted
2 tablespoons brown sugar
1/2 cup granulated sugar
12 large graham crackers

Combine the pecans, 1 tablespoon of the butter and the brown sugar in a bowl and mix well. Spread on a baking sheet. Bake at 325 degrees for 5 to 10 minutes or until toasted, stirring once. Combine the remaining butter and the granulated sugar in a small saucepan. Bring to a boil and boil for 2 minutes, stirring frequently. Arrange the graham crackers in a 10×15-inch baking pan sprayed with cooking spray. Pour the butter mixture evenly over the crackers. Sprinkle with the pecans. Bake at 325 degrees for 10 to 12 minutes or until golden brown. Remove immediately to waxed paper. Let cool. Break into small pieces.

Yield: 4 dozen cookies

Mary Claire's Mud and Mint Bites

1 (15-ounce) package brownie mix
1/3 cup hot water
1/4 cup vegetable oil
1 egg
48 miniature chocolate mint patties

Combine the brownie mix, water, oil and egg in a bowl and mix well with a spoon. Fill paper-lined miniature muffin cups one-half full with the batter. Press the chocolate mint patties gently into the batter. Bake at 350 degrees for 15 minutes.

Yield: 48 servings

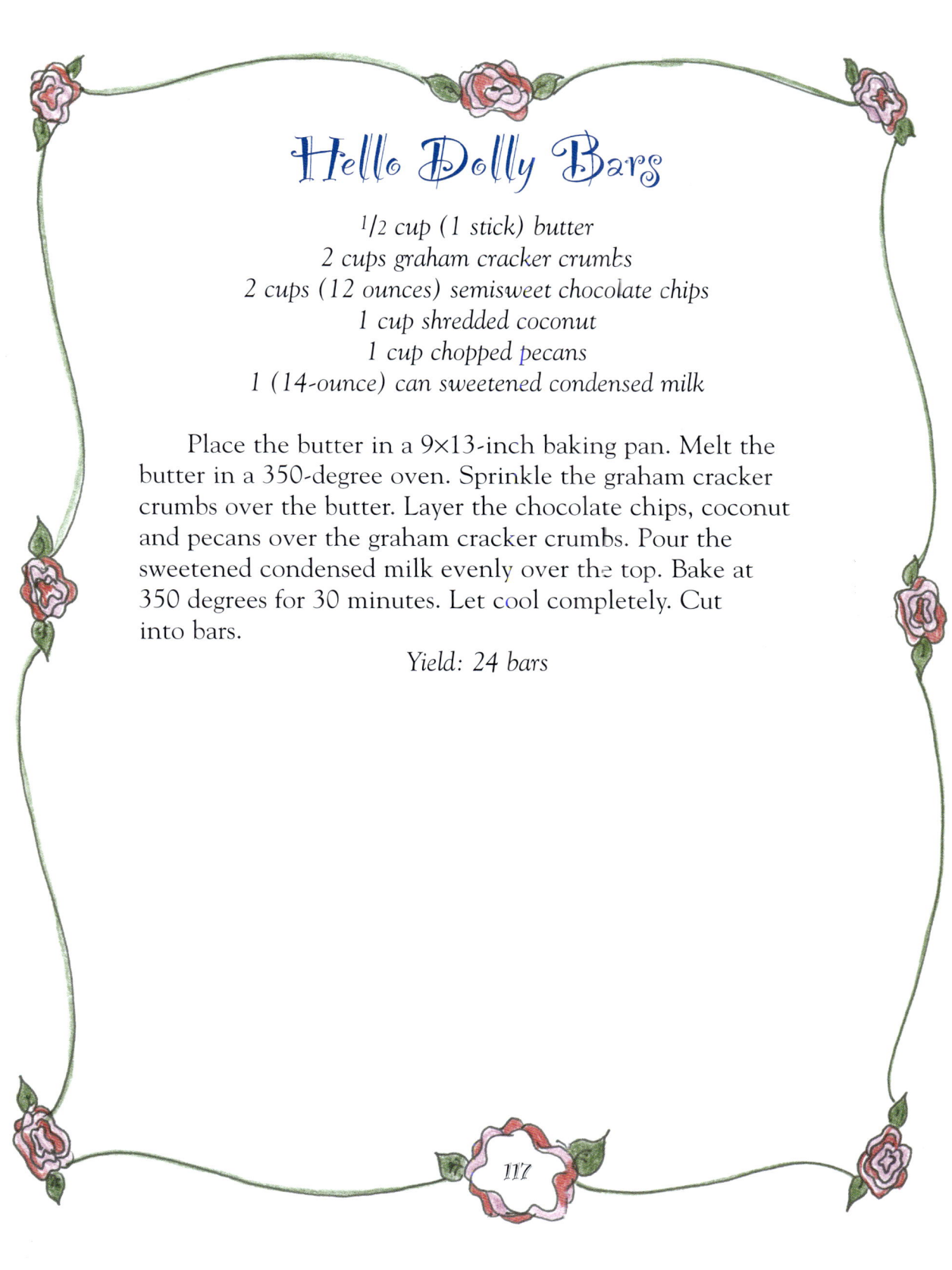

Hello Dolly Bars

1/2 cup (1 stick) butter
2 cups graham cracker crumbs
2 cups (12 ounces) semisweet chocolate chips
1 cup shredded coconut
1 cup chopped pecans
1 (14-ounce) can sweetened condensed milk

Place the butter in a 9×13-inch baking pan. Melt the butter in a 350-degree oven. Sprinkle the graham cracker crumbs over the butter. Layer the chocolate chips, coconut and pecans over the graham cracker crumbs. Pour the sweetened condensed milk evenly over the top. Bake at 350 degrees for 30 minutes. Let cool completely. Cut into bars.

Yield: 24 bars

Out-of-this-World Lemon Squares

1/2 cup (1 stick) butter, softened
1/2 cup confectioners' sugar
1 cup all-purpose flour
Pinch of salt
2 eggs
1 cup granulated sugar
2 to 3 tablespoons lemon juice
Grated zest of 1/4 lemon
1 cup confectioners' sugar
1 tablespoon butter, softened
Lemon juice

Combine 1/2 cup butter, 1/2 cup confectioners' sugar, the flour and salt in a bowl and mix well. Press over the bottom of a 9×13-inch baking dish. Bake at 350 degrees for 15 to 20 minutes or until light brown. Combine the eggs, granulated sugar, 2 to 3 tablespoons lemon juice and the lemon zest in a bowl and beat until blended. Pour over the baked layer. Bake at 350 degrees for 20 to 25 minutes or until set. Let cool completely. Combine 1 cup confectioners' sugar and 1 tablespoon butter in a bowl and mix well. Stir in enough lemon juice to reach a spreading consistency. Spread over the cooled squares.

Yield: 24 servings

Chess Cake Bars

1 (2-layer) package yellow cake mix
1 egg, lightly beaten
$1/2$ cup (1 stick) butter or margarine, softened
$3/4$ to 1 cup chopped pecans
8 ounces cream cheese, softened
2 eggs
1 teaspoon vanilla extract
$3^3/4$ cups confectioners' sugar

Combine the cake mix and 1 egg in a bowl and mix well. Cut in the butter with a pastry blender until crumbly. Press over the bottom of a well-greased 9×13-inch baking pan. Sprinkle with the pecans. Combine the cream cheese, 2 eggs, vanilla and confectioners' sugar in a mixing bowl and beat for 3 to 5 minutes or until blended. Spread over the pecans. Bake at 350 degrees for 40 to 50 minutes or until golden brown. Sprinkle with additional confectioners' sugar. Cut into squares while still warm using a damp knife. Let stand at room temperature or chill until firm.

Yield: 24 servings

Raw Fruit

Fruit such as apples and pears should be quartered and cored, then eaten with your fingers. Grapes should be eaten with your fingers. Whole strawberries, when served as a dessert with whipped cream, may require a fork or a spoon and some cutting. Hold a berry with your fork, then cut and eat it with your spoon.

Simple Shortbread

1/2 cup sugar
1/2 teaspoon salt
1 cup (2 sticks) chilled unsalted butter
1/4 teaspoon vanilla extract
2 cups all-purpose flour

Combine the sugar and salt in a food processor. Add the butter and pulse until the mixture is smooth. Add the vanilla and process until blended. Add the flour and process until slightly crumbly. Shape the dough into a ball and wrap in plastic wrap. Chill for 30 minutes. Press the dough in a 10×15-inch baking pan sprayed with baking spray with flour. Bake at 250 degrees for 30 minutes or until light golden brown. Cut into squares while still warm. Let cool in the pan.

Yield: 24 servings

Pizza Cookie

1 (18-ounce) package
chocolate chip cookie dough
$3/4$ cup chocolate chips
$3/4$ cup peanut butter chips
3 Snickers candy bars, chopped
$1/2$ cup "M & M's" Miniature
Chocolate Candies

Spread the cookie dough $1/4$ inch thick on a large pizza pan. Bake at 350 degrees until almost done. Sprinkle with the chocolate chips and peanut butter chips. Bake for 2 to 3 minutes or until the edge of the cookie dough is golden brown and the chocolate and peanut butter chips are melted. Spread the chocolate and peanut butter chips evenly over the baked layer. Sprinkle with the chopped candy bars and chocolate candies.

Yield: 16 slices

Fabulous Fudge

1 (7-ounce) jar marshmallow creme
2 (12-ounce) packages milk chocolate kisses
5 cups sugar
1 (13-ounce) can evaporated milk
1/2 cup (1 stick) butter
6 cups coarsely chopped pecans

Combine the marshmallow creme and chocolate kisses in a large bowl. Combine the sugar, evaporated milk and butter in a saucepan. Bring to a rolling boil and boil for 7 to 8 minutes, stirring constantly. Pour over the chocolate kiss mixture and stir with a wooden spoon. Stir in the pecans. Pour into two generously buttered 9×13-inch pans. Let cool completely and cut into squares. You may use crispy rice cereal instead of pecans.

Yield: 6 dozen pieces

Peanut Butter Balls

1 cup peanut butter
$1/2$ cup (1 stick) butter, softened
2 cups confectioners' sugar
1 (24-ounce) package chocolate almond bark

Mix the first 3 ingredients in a bowl. Shape into balls and place on a tray. Freeze until firm. Melt the bark in a double boiler. Dip the peanut butter balls in the melted bark and place on a tray. Freeze until firm. Store in an airtight container.

Yield: 3 dozen balls

Nana and Paw Paw's Green Stuff

1 prepared angel food cake, torn into pieces
2 (6-ounce) packages pistachio instant pudding mix, prepared
12 ounces whipped topping
$1/2$ (14-ounce) package chocolate sandwich cookies, crushed

Place the cake pieces in a 9×13-inch pan. Pour the pudding over the cake pieces. Spread with the whipped topping. Sprinkle with the cookies. Chill, covered, for 2 to 3 hours.

Yield: 15 to 20 servings

Serving

When serving yourself, take only the amount of food you know you can eat. When serving yourself from a platter with a serving fork and spoon, put the spoon under the food and use the fork to hold it in place as you put it on your plate. When a hostess serves you, you should try a few bites of each dish. You may discover some new favorite foods. To serve yourself from a condiment (ketchup, mustard, relish, etc.) or jelly dish, use the serving spoon to place a helping on your plate.

Grilled Pound Cake S'mores

1 (10-ounce) frozen pound cake, thawed
1 cup marshmallow creme
1 cup (6 ounces) semisweet chocolate chips
Vanilla ice cream, softened (optional)

Slice the pound cake horizontally into three layers. Place the bottom layer on a large sheet of heavy-duty foil. Spread with 1/2 cup of the marshmallow creme. Sprinkle with 1/2 cup of the chocolate chips. Repeat the procedure with the remaining ingredients, ending with the top cake layer. Enclose with the foil, folding the edges to seal. Grill over low heat for 7 to 10 minutes or until warm. Slice and serve immediately with ice cream.

Yield: 6 servings

Apple Dumplings

1/2 cup sugar
1 teaspoon ground cinnamon
3/4 cup (1 1/2 sticks) butter
1 cup sugar
1/2 cup orange juice
2 tablespoons vanilla extract
1 (8-count) can crescent rolls
2 Granny Smith apples, peeled and quartered

Combine 1/2 cup sugar and the cinnamon in a small bowl. Melt the butter in a saucepan. Add 1 cup sugar and the orange juice and bring to a boil, stirring frequently. Stir in the vanilla. Remove from the heat. Separate the crescent roll dough into triangles. Place an apple section in the center of each triangle. Sprinkle with some of the cinnamon-sugar mixture. Roll up the dough to enclose the filling. Arrange seam side down in an 8 1/2×11-inch baking pan or a 9×13-inch baking pan. Pour the butter mixture over the rolls. Sprinkle with the remaining cinnamon-sugar mixture. Bake at 350 degrees for 35 minutes.

Yield: 8 servings

Do not put condiments or jelly directly onto your food. French fries should be dipped into ketchup, not covered with it. Condiments may be put directly onto sandwiches.
If condiments, crackers, butter, etc., are served in a paper wrapper at a casual restaurant, remove the wrappers and place them under the rim of your plate.
In a fast food restaurant, place empty wrappers neatly on your tray or napkin.

125

Hot Lava Pudding

1 cup sifted all-purpose flour
3/4 cup sugar
2 tablespoons baking cocoa
2 teaspoons baking powder
1/4 teaspoon salt
1/2 cup milk
2 tablespoons shortening, melted
1 cup chopped nuts
1 cup packed brown sugar
1/4 cup baking cocoa
1 3/4 cups hot water

Sift the flour, sugar, 2 tablespoons baking cocoa, the baking powder and salt together in a bowl. Stir in the milk and shortening until blended. Stir in the nuts. Spread in a 9×9-inch baking pan. Combine the brown sugar and 1/4 cup baking cocoa. Sprinkle over the prepared layer. Pour hot water over the top. Bake at 350 degrees for 45 minutes. The cake mixture will rise to the top and the chocolate sauce will settle to the bottom during the baking process.

Yield: 8 to 10 servings

Peppermint Mousse

1 cup milk
4 ounces peppermint candy
1 teaspoon unflavored gelatin
2 tablespoons cold water
1 tablespoon vanilla extract
1/8 teaspoon salt
1 cup whipped cream

Heat the milk in a small saucepan over low heat. Add the peppermint candy and heat until the candy dissolves, stirring frequently. Remove from the heat. Dissolve the gelatin in the cold water in a small bowl. Add to the peppermint mixture. Stir in the vanilla and salt. Chill in the refrigerator until the mixture is stiff. Fold in the whipped cream. Serve in chocolate shells, if desired.

Yield: 12 to 15 servings

Holidays

New Year's Bubbly
Gelatin Parfait

President's Day
Cherry Delight

Valentine Peppermint
Hearts

Valentine Peppermint
Marshmallows

Cranberry Sweetheart
Scones

St. Pat's Irish Soda Bread

Easter Egg Nests

Resurrection Rolls

April Fool's Grilled Cheese

Cinco de Mayo Pralines

Mother's Day "Tea Party"
Minted Lemon Tea

Mother's Day Jammies

Pop's Poppin' Corn

Fourth of July Confetti
Ice Cream Pops

Fourth of July
Fruit Salad

Ghost Suckers

Halloween Hands

Halloween Pumpkin Brew

Spooky Spaghetti
with Meatballs

Breakfast Acorns

Turkey Cookies

Hanukkah Potato Latkes

Gingerbread

Stained Glass Cookies

Christmas Trees

"Santa" Tarts

Aaron's Christmas Punch

Kwanzaa Bread Pudding

New Year's Bubbly Gelatin Parfait

1 (3-ounce) package sparkling white grape gelatin
Club soda, seltzer water or ginger ale

Make the gelatin using the package directions for preparing with club soda. Pour into champagne flutes or parfait glasses. Chill until set. Prepare these the day you will be serving them or the gelatin may loose its bubbles.

Yield: 4 servings

President's Day Cherry Delight

2 cups graham cracker crumbs
1/2 cup (1 stick) butter, melted
1 cup confectioners' sugar
8 ounces cream cheese, softened
2 tablespoons milk
1 (21-ounce) can cherry pie filling or
your favorite flavor pie filling

Combine the graham cracker crumbs and butter in a bowl and mix well. Press over the bottom of a 9×13-inch baking pan. Bake at 375 degrees for 8 to 12 minutes or until golden brown. Let stand until cool. Combine the confectioners' sugar, cream cheese and milk in a mixing bowl and beat until blended. Spread over the baked layer. Top with the pie filling. Chill, covered, for 2 to 3 hours before serving.

Yield: 15 servings

Table Settings

Dishes, flatware, and glasses are put together in place settings. They can be very simple for casual dining—like dinner at home on Tuesday night—or very fancy for ormal dining, like Thanksgiving dinner or a meal in a fine restaurant. Refer to page 169 for table settings.

Valentine Peppermint Hearts

18 (2^1/$_2$-inch) candy canes
5 ounces vanilla almond bark, chopped
2 teaspoons crushed peppermint candies

Line a baking sheet with waxed paper. Arrange two of the candy canes with the ends touching so that they form a heart on the waxed paper. Repeat with the remaining candy canes. Place the almond bark in a microwave-safe bowl. Microwave on Medium for 2 to 3 minutes or until melted, stirring once. Spoon or pipe the melted almond bark into the center of the hearts, filling the space. Sprinkle with the crushed peppermint candies. Let stand for 30 minutes or until set.

Yield: 9 hearts

Valentine
Peppermint Marshmallows

3/4 cup confectioners' sugar
1 teaspoon peppermint extract
1 (10-ounce) package miniature marshmallows

Combine the confectioners' sugar and peppermint extract in a sealable plastic bag. Add the marshmallows and shake vigorously to coat. Use these in hot chocolate for a peppermint treat.

Yield: 12 servings

133

Cranberry Sweetheart Scones

2 cups all-purpose flour
1 tablespoon granulated sugar
2 teaspoons baking powder
1/2 teaspoon salt
1/4 cup (1/2 stick) butter
1 teaspoon grated orange zest
1 cup chopped fresh cranberries or
sweetened dried cranberries
2 eggs
1/2 cup milk
1/4 to 1/2 cup raw sugar

Combine the flour, granulated sugar, baking powder and
salt in a bowl. Cut in the butter with a pastry blender until
crumbly. Add the orange zest and cranberries and stir gently.
Combine the eggs and milk in a mixing bowl and beat until
blended. Add to the cranberry mixture and stir just until
combined. Knead the dough a few times on a lightly floured
surface. Pat to 1-inch thickness. Cut into heart shapes.
Arrange on an ungreased baking sheet. Sprinkle evenly with
the raw sugar. Bake at 400 degrees for 12 to 15 minutes or
until light golden brown.

Yield: 8 to 10 servings

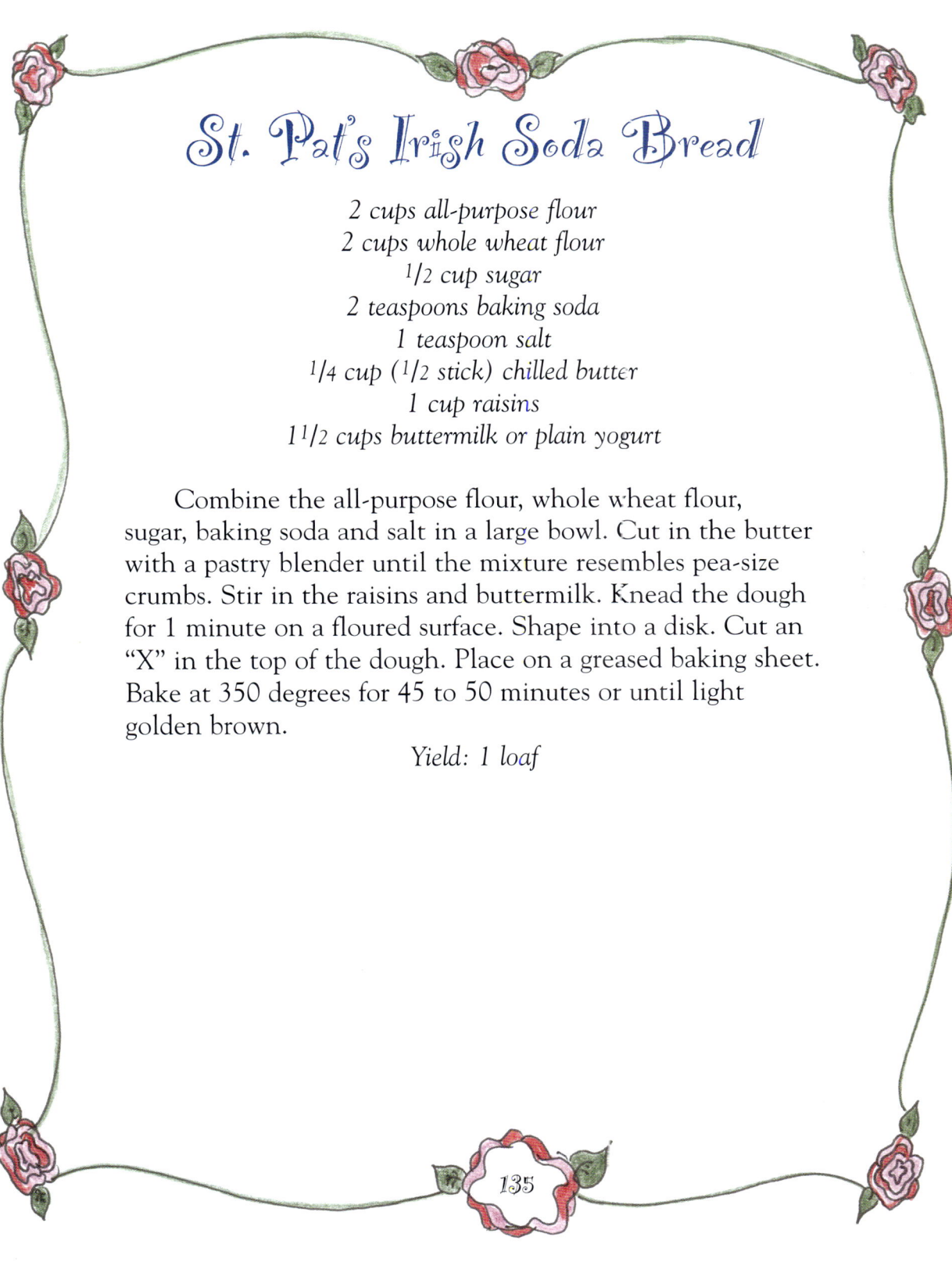

St. Pat's Irish Soda Bread

2 cups all-purpose flour
2 cups whole wheat flour
1/2 cup sugar
2 teaspoons baking soda
1 teaspoon salt
1/4 cup (1/2 stick) chilled butter
1 cup raisins
1 1/2 cups buttermilk or plain yogurt

Combine the all-purpose flour, whole wheat flour, sugar, baking soda and salt in a large bowl. Cut in the butter with a pastry blender until the mixture resembles pea-size crumbs. Stir in the raisins and buttermilk. Knead the dough for 1 minute on a floured surface. Shape into a disk. Cut an "X" in the top of the dough. Place on a greased baking sheet. Bake at 350 degrees for 45 to 50 minutes or until light golden brown.

Yield: 1 loaf

Unwanted Bites

When you discover a seed, pit, or bone in the food you are eating, chew as much meat from it as possible, and then take it from your mouth with your thumb and pointer finger of a cupped hand. Do the same with gristle, but remove it from your mouth with your fork or spoon. Place it on the side of your plate.

Easter Egg Nests

1 (12-ounce) bag butterscotch chips
1/2 cup peanut butter
1 (12-ounce) bag chow mein noodles
1 (14-ounce) bag speckled jelly beans

Combine the butterscotch chips and peanut butter in a large saucepan. Cook over low heat until the butterscotch chips are melted and the mixture is smooth, stirring constantly. Add the chow mein noodles and stir gently to coat. Drop small amounts of the mixture onto a greased baking sheet to form nests. Top each nest with two or three jelly beans. Let stand for 10 to 15 minutes. Store in an airtight container.

Yield: 5 1/2 dozen nests

Resurrection Rolls

1 (8-count) can crescent rolls
8 large marshmallows
1/4 cup (1/2 stick) butter, melted
3 to 4 tablespoons cinnamon-sugar

Separate the crescent roll dough into triangles. Roll the marshmallows in the butter. Roll in the cinnamon-sugar to coat. Wrap each coated marshmallow in a dough triangle, shaping into a ball and pressing the edges to seal tightly. Arrange the dough balls on a baking sheet. Bake at 350 degrees for 10 to 12 minutes or until light golden brown. Let cool slightly. You will find that each roll is empty inside (empty tomb) and the marshmallow has disappeared. (Where is it?)

Yield: 8 rolls

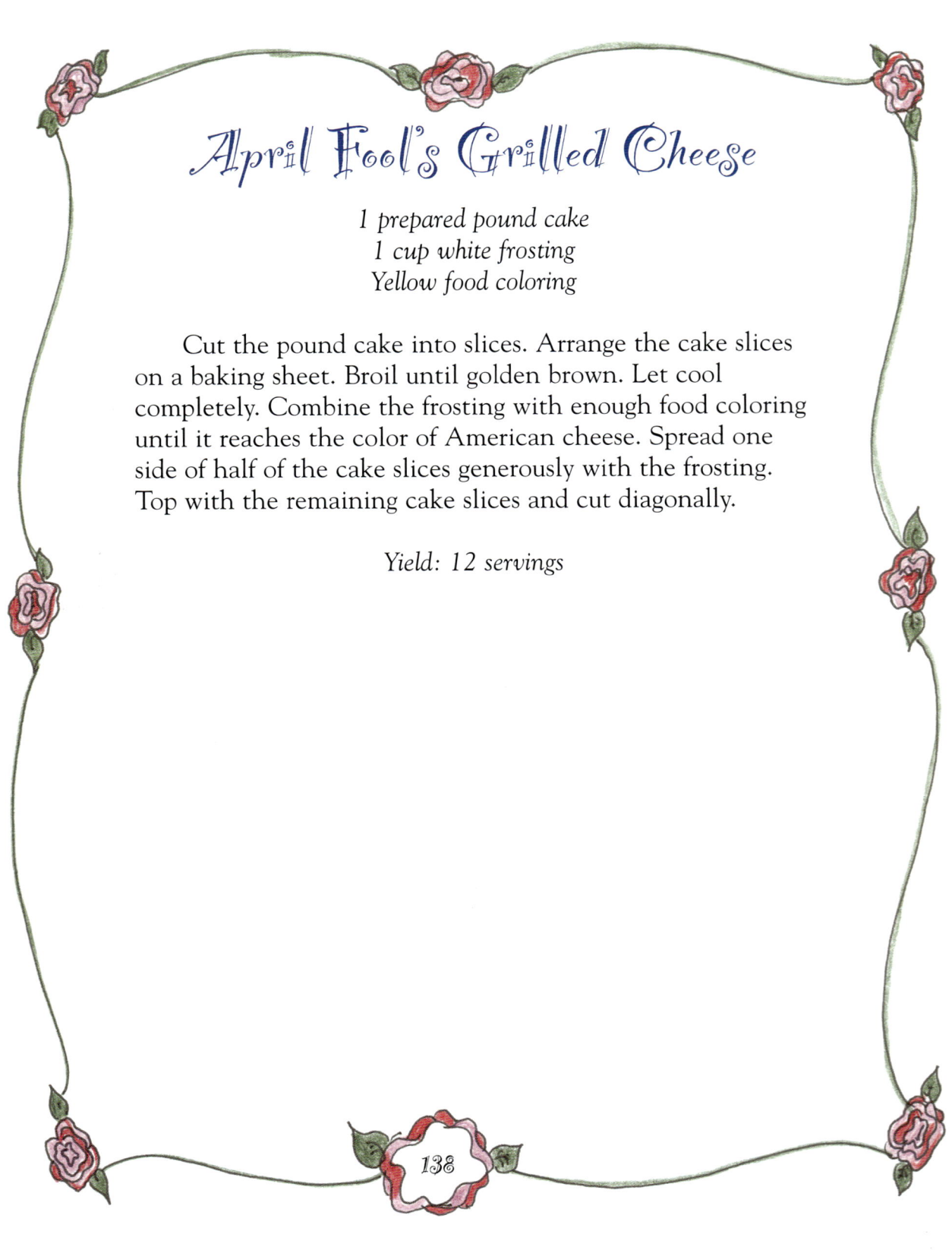

April Fool's Grilled Cheese

1 prepared pound cake
1 cup white frosting
Yellow food coloring

Cut the pound cake into slices. Arrange the cake slices on a baking sheet. Broil until golden brown. Let cool completely. Combine the frosting with enough food coloring until it reaches the color of American cheese. Spread one side of half of the cake slices generously with the frosting. Top with the remaining cake slices and cut diagonally.

Yield: 12 servings

Cinco de Mayo Pralines

1 1/4 cups granulated sugar
3/4 cup packed brown sugar
1/2 cup evaporated milk
1/4 cup (1/2 stick) butter, frozen
1 tablespoon vanilla extract
1 1/2 cups pecan pieces

Combine the granulated sugar, brown sugar and evaporated milk in a saucepan. Cook over medium heat to 234 to 240 degrees on a candy thermometer, soft-ball stage, stirring frequently. Remove from the heat. Add the butter, vanilla and pecans and stir until no longer shiny. Drop by spoonfuls onto waxed paper. Let stand until set. Store in an airtight container.

Yield: 20 servings

Mother's Day
"Tea Party" Minted Lemon Tea

4 cups boiling water
4 family-size tea bags
$^1/_2$ cup loosely packed fresh mint leaves
$^3/_4$ cup sugar
1 (6-ounce) can frozen lemonade concentrate
4 cups cold water

Pour the boiling water over the tea bags and mint leaves into a large pitcher. Let steep, covered, for 3 minutes. Remove and discard the tea bags and mint leaves. Add the sugar and stir until dissolved. Stir in the lemonade concentrate and the cold water. Chill until ready to serve. Pour into ice-filled glasses and garnish with mint leaves and lemon slices.

Yield: 9 cups

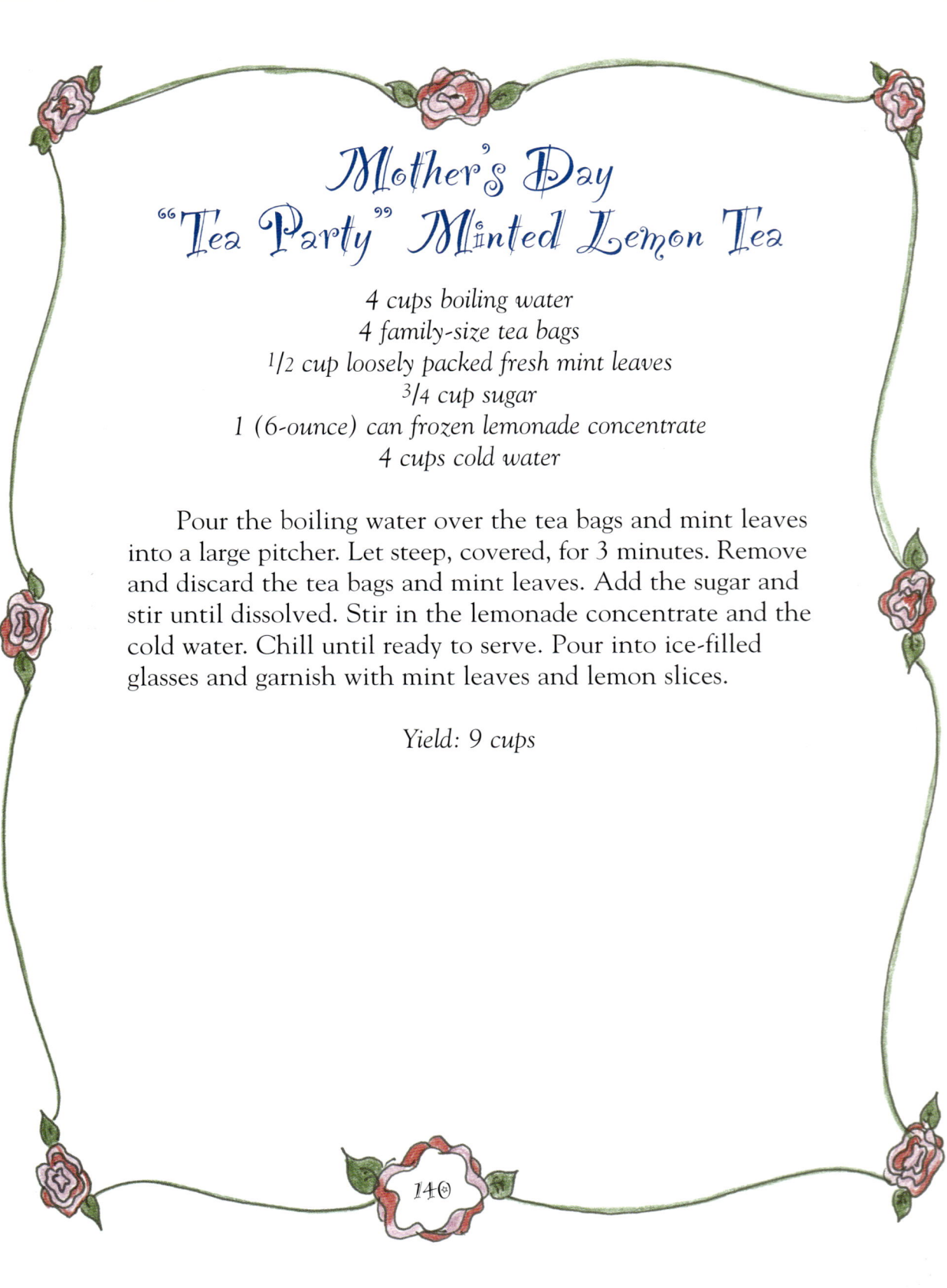

Mother's Day Jammies

1 (9-inch) pie pastry
Your favorite flavor jam or preserves
1 cup confectioners' sugar
1 1/2 tablespoons water

Unfold the pastry onto a lightly floured surface. Spread a thin layer of jam over the pastry. Cut into twenty wedges. Roll each wedge starting at the wide edge. Chill for 1 hour. Arrange the rolls on a baking sheet lined with greased foil. Bake at 450 degrees for 10 to 12 minutes or until light brown. Combine the confectioners' sugar and water in a bowl and mix well. Drizzle over the warm rolls.

Yield: 20 servings

Pop's Poppin' Corn

8 cups popped popcorn
2 tablespoons butter, melted
1/2 cup (2 ounces) grated Parmesan cheese
1 teaspoon mild chili powder
Salt to taste

Mix all the ingredients in a large bowl and toss gently to coat. Serve immediately or store in an airtight container.

Yield: 6 servings

Vegetables

Vegetables should be eaten with a fork or spoon. If necessary, cut up larger pieces with a knife. Remember, cut up just one or two bites at a time. You may use a small piece of bread to help push those last few peas or carrots onto your fork.

Fourth of July Confetti Ice Cream Pops

8 (1^1/2-inch) pieces soft-centered candy bars, such as Milky Way or Snickers
1 pint vanilla ice cream, slightly softened
^{3}/4 cup red, white and blue candy confetti or candy sprinkles

Insert a wooden popsicle stick into one end of each candy bar piece. Spoon 1 tablespoon of the ice cream into a 3-ounce paper cup. Place a candy piece in the center of the cup. Cover the candy with about 3 tablespoons of the ice cream, smoothing the top. Repeat with the remaining ice cream and candy. Place on a tray. Freeze until solid. Peel the paper cups from the ice cream pops. Roll the ice cream pops in the candy confetti. Store in the freezer for up to 3 days.

Yield: 8 servings

Fourth of July Fruit Salad

1/4 cup fresh lime juice
1/4 cup honey
2 tablespoons chopped fresh mint
3 cups fresh blueberries
1 quart fresh strawberries, cut into halves
3 apples, peeled and cut into 1-inch pieces

Combine the lime juice, honey and mint in a large bowl and mix well. Add the blueberries, strawberries and apples and toss gently to coat. Let stand for 15 minutes or longer. Serve with ice cream for a delicious dessert.

Yield: 8 servings

Ghost Suckers

1 (6-ounce) package white almond bark
Candy sucker sticks
1 cup (6 ounces) chocolate chips

Melt the white almond bark using the package directions. Line a baking sheet or tray with foil. Arrange candy sucker sticks four inches apart on the prepared baking sheet. Spoon the white almond bark in ghost shapes over the candy sticks. Place two chocolate chips on each ghost for the eyes. Chill in the refrigerator until hard. Wrap each sucker in plastic wrap.

Yield: variable

Halloween Hands

Candy corn
6 clear food handlers gloves
8 cups popped popcorn
Orange or black ribbon
6 spider rings

Place three candy corn pieces in the end of each glove finger. Fill the gloves with popcorn. Tie the glove at the wrist with ribbon. Place a spider ring on one of the fingers.

Yield: 6 hands

Halloween
Pumpkin Brew

2 cups apple cider
2 cups vanilla ice cream
2 tablespoons honey
1/2 teaspoon ground cinnamon
1/4 teaspoon ground nutmeg

Combine the apple cider, ice cream, honey, cinnamon and nutmeg in a blender and process until smooth. Serve in frosted mugs. You may add orange food coloring and freeze plastic spiders in ice cubes to float in the brew.

Yield: 4 servings

Spooky Spaghetti with Meatballs

3 pounds lean ground beef
1 tablespoon oregano
1 tablespoon parsley
1 garlic clove, chopped
1 envelope dry onion soup mix
2 cups Italian-style bread crumbs
Green olives
2 (16-ounce) jars of your favorite spaghetti sauce
Spaghetti, cooked and drained

Combine the ground beef, oregano, parsley and garlic in a bowl and mix well. Add the onion soup mix and bread crumbs and mix well. Shape the mixture into balls. Place a green olive with the pimento side up to resemble an eye on each meatball. Arrange in a lightly greased 10×15-inch baking pan. Bake at 350 degrees for 1 hour or until the meatballs are brown and cooked through. Combine the spaghetti sauce and pasta in a large saucepan and bring to a simmer. Spoon the spaghetti and sauce onto a large serving platter. Top with the meatballs.

Yield: 8 servings

Breakfast Acorns

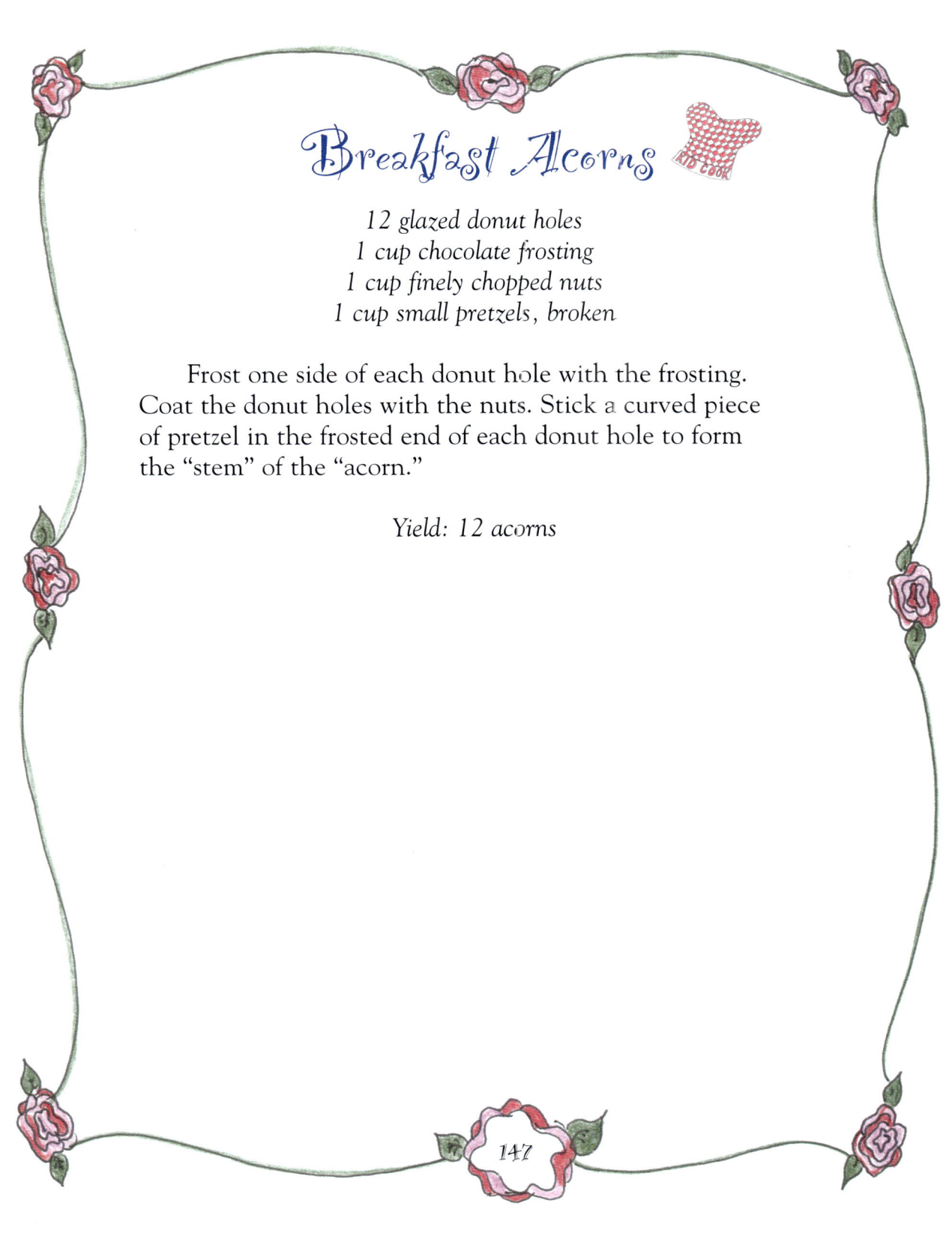

12 glazed donut holes
1 cup chocolate frosting
1 cup finely chopped nuts
1 cup small pretzels, broken

Frost one side of each donut hole with the frosting. Coat the donut holes with the nuts. Stick a curved piece of pretzel in the frosted end of each donut hole to form the "stem" of the "acorn."

Yield: 12 acorns

Turkey Cookies

12 pinwheel cookies
12 fudge stripe cookies
1 (16-ounce) can chocolate frosting
12 malted milk balls
12 pieces candy corn

Cut off half of the back of each pinwheel cookie. Attach a fudge stripe cookie to the cut side of the pinwheel to form the tail of the turkey using the frosting as glue and making sure that the stripes are vertical. Attach a malted milk ball to the front of each pinwheel cookie to form the head of the turkey using the frosting as glue. Add a candy corn to each malted milk ball to form a beak using the frosting as glue. You may have to press and hold each piece in place for a few seconds to allow the frosting to set.

Yield: 12 turkeys

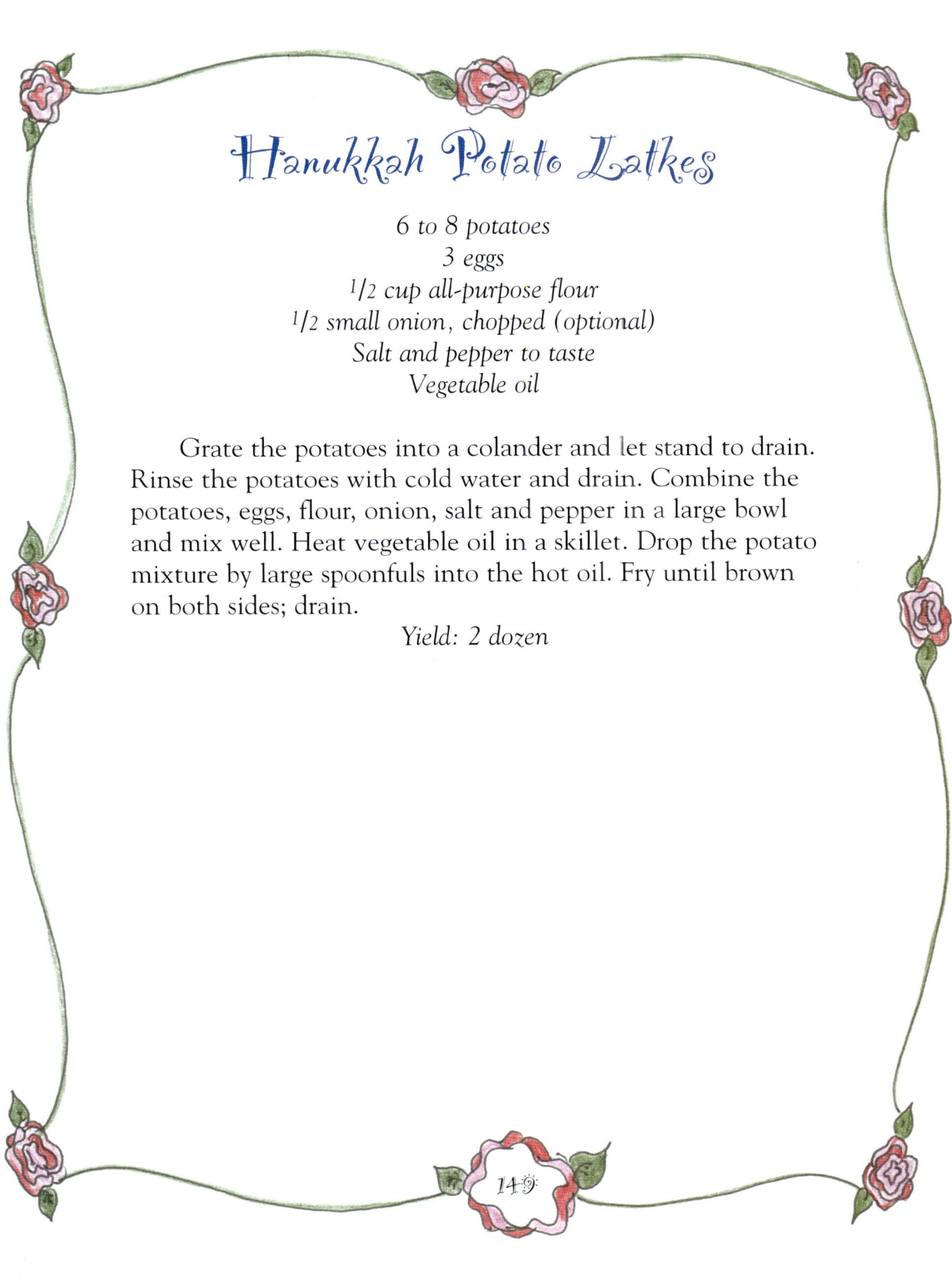

Hanukkah Potato Latkes

6 to 8 potatoes
3 eggs
$1/2$ cup all-purpose flour
$1/2$ small onion, chopped (optional)
Salt and pepper to taste
Vegetable oil

Grate the potatoes into a colander and let stand to drain. Rinse the potatoes with cold water and drain. Combine the potatoes, eggs, flour, onion, salt and pepper in a large bowl and mix well. Heat vegetable oil in a skillet. Drop the potato mixture by large spoonfuls into the hot oil. Fry until brown on both sides; drain.

Yield: 2 dozen

Wait to Begin Eating

You should wait until everyone is seated and served before you begin eating. At a party, you should always wait for the hostess or birthday boy/girl to lift his/her fork.

Gingerbread

1 cup (2 sticks) butter or margarine
1 cup sugar
2 eggs
2$\frac{1}{2}$ cups all-purpose flour
1 teaspoon baking soda
1 teaspoon ginger
1 teaspoon ground cinnamon
1 teaspoon ground cloves
1 teaspoon ground allspice
1 cup molasses
1 cup boiling water

Cream the butter and sugar in a mixing bowl until light and fluffy. Add the eggs one at a time, beating well after each addition. Add the flour, baking soda, ginger, cinnamon, cloves and allspice and mix well. Add the molasses and water and mix well. Pour into a greased 9×13-inch baking pan. Bake at 350 degrees for 45 minutes.

Yield: 15 servings

Stained Glass Cookies

2 (18-ounce) packages sugar cookie dough
4 (7-ounce) packages hard candies,
such as Jolly Ranchers in
assorted colors, broken

Roll the cookie dough to $1/2$-inch thickness on a floured surface or waxed paper. Cut the dough with holiday-themed cookie cutters. Place the cookies on a cookie sheet sprayed with nonstick cooking spray. Cut a hole in the center of each cookie and fill the hole with candy pieces. Poke the top of each cookie with a skewer to make a $1/4$-inch hole. Bake at 350 degrees for 8 minutes or until the candy is melted and the cookies are light brown. Cool for 5 minutes on the cookie sheet. Remove to a wire rack to cool completely. Tie a ribbon through the hole in each cookie and hang from your tree if the kids don't eat them first!

Yield: about 48 cookies

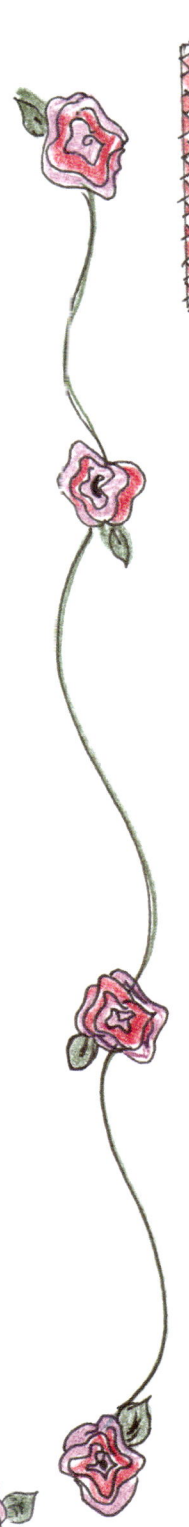

Christmas Trees

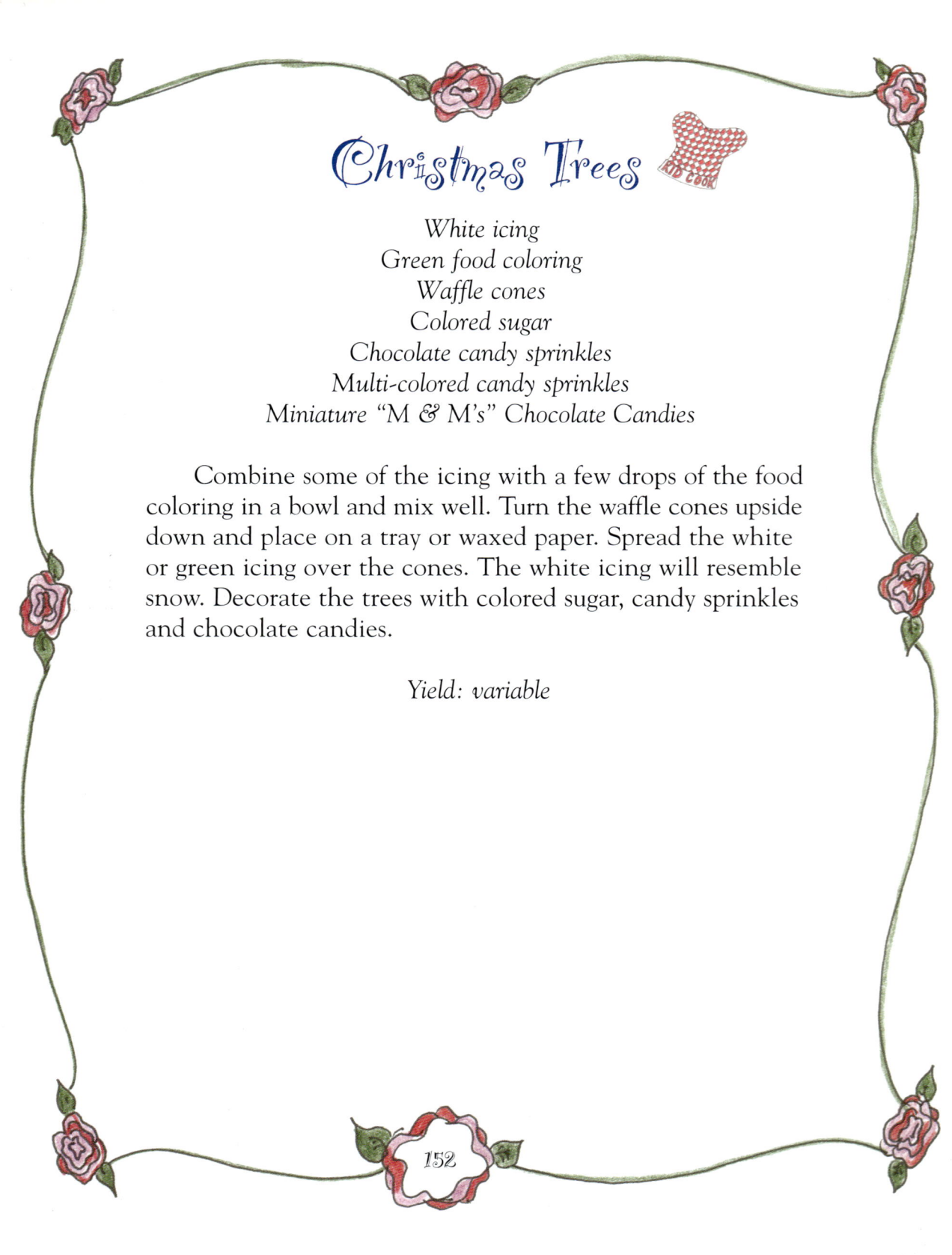

White icing
Green food coloring
Waffle cones
Colored sugar
Chocolate candy sprinkles
Multi-colored candy sprinkles
Miniature "M & M's" Chocolate Candies

Combine some of the icing with a few drops of the food coloring in a bowl and mix well. Turn the waffle cones upside down and place on a tray or waxed paper. Spread the white or green icing over the cones. The white icing will resemble snow. Decorate the trees with colored sugar, candy sprinkles and chocolate candies.

Yield: variable

"Santa" Tarts

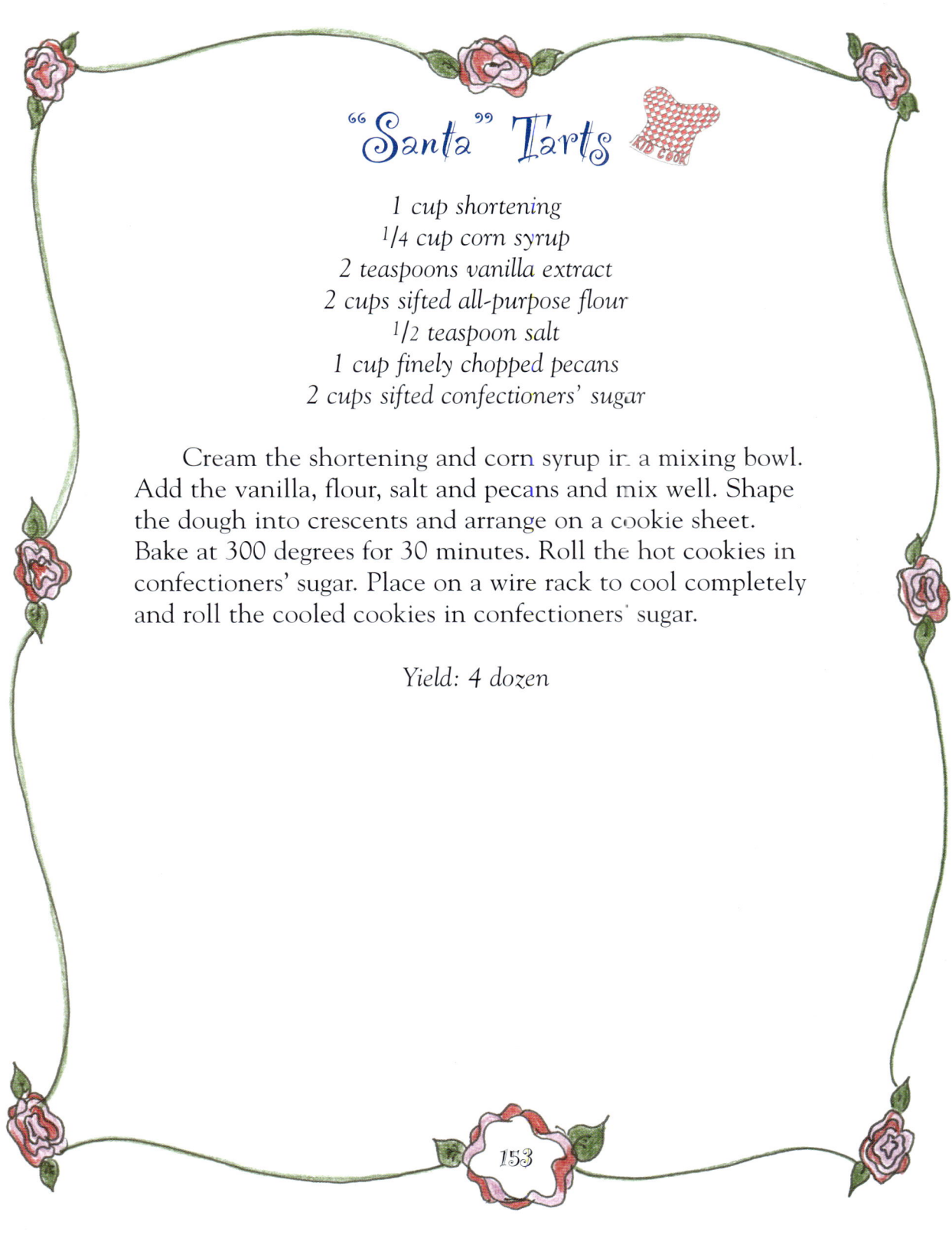

1 cup shortening
1/4 cup corn syrup
2 teaspoons vanilla extract
2 cups sifted all-purpose flour
1/2 teaspoon salt
1 cup finely chopped pecans
2 cups sifted confectioners' sugar

Cream the shortening and corn syrup in a mixing bowl. Add the vanilla, flour, salt and pecans and mix well. Shape the dough into crescents and arrange on a cookie sheet. Bake at 300 degrees for 30 minutes. Roll the hot cookies in confectioners' sugar. Place on a wire rack to cool completely and roll the cooled cookies in confectioners' sugar.

Yield: 4 dozen

eXcuse me

*You should always
ask to be excused
from the table if you
need to leave or get
up for any reason—
whether it is to go to
the bathroom, get
something in the
kitchen, or if you are
finished eating
your meal.*

Aaron's Christmas Punch

*1 (46-ounce) can pineapple juice
1 (46-ounce) can apple juice or cranapple juice
1 (12-ounce) can frozen pink
lemonade concentrate
1/2 cup sugar
4 (2-liter) bottles chilled ginger ale, or to taste*

Combine the pineapple juice, apple juice, lemonade concentrate and sugar in a large container and stir until the sugar dissolves. Place in the freezer for several hours to overnight. Remove from the freezer 3 to 4 hours before serving to allow the mixture to become slushy. Break up the mixture and pour into a punch bowl. Add the ginger ale just before serving. Do not add ice. The more ginger ale added, the sweeter the punch.

Yield: 40 (6-ounce) servings

154

Kwanzaa Bread Pudding

6 eggs
4 cups milk
4 cups sugar, or to taste
1/2 teaspoon nutmeg
2 1/2 teaspoons vanilla extract
1 large loaf, or 2 small loaves,
good quality white bread, cubed
1 (16-ounce) can peaches,
drained and finely chopped
2 cups raisins
1/4 cup (1/2 stick) butter, chopped
1/2 teaspoon nutmeg

Combine the eggs and milk in a bowl and whisk until blended. Add the sugar, 1/2 teaspoon nutmeg and the vanilla and mix well. Arrange the bread cubes in a 9×13-inch baking pan. Place the peaches and raisins between the bread cubes, pressing the raisins down. Pour the egg mixture over the bread and fruit. The pan will be very full. Top with the butter and sprinkle with 1/2 teaspoon nutmeg. Bake at 375 degrees for 40 to 60 minutes or until brown. Serve warm with whipped cream or vanilla ice cream.

Yield: 12 servings

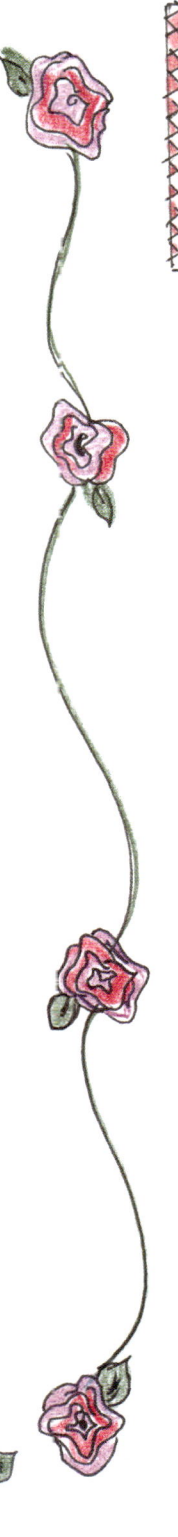

Food Crafts

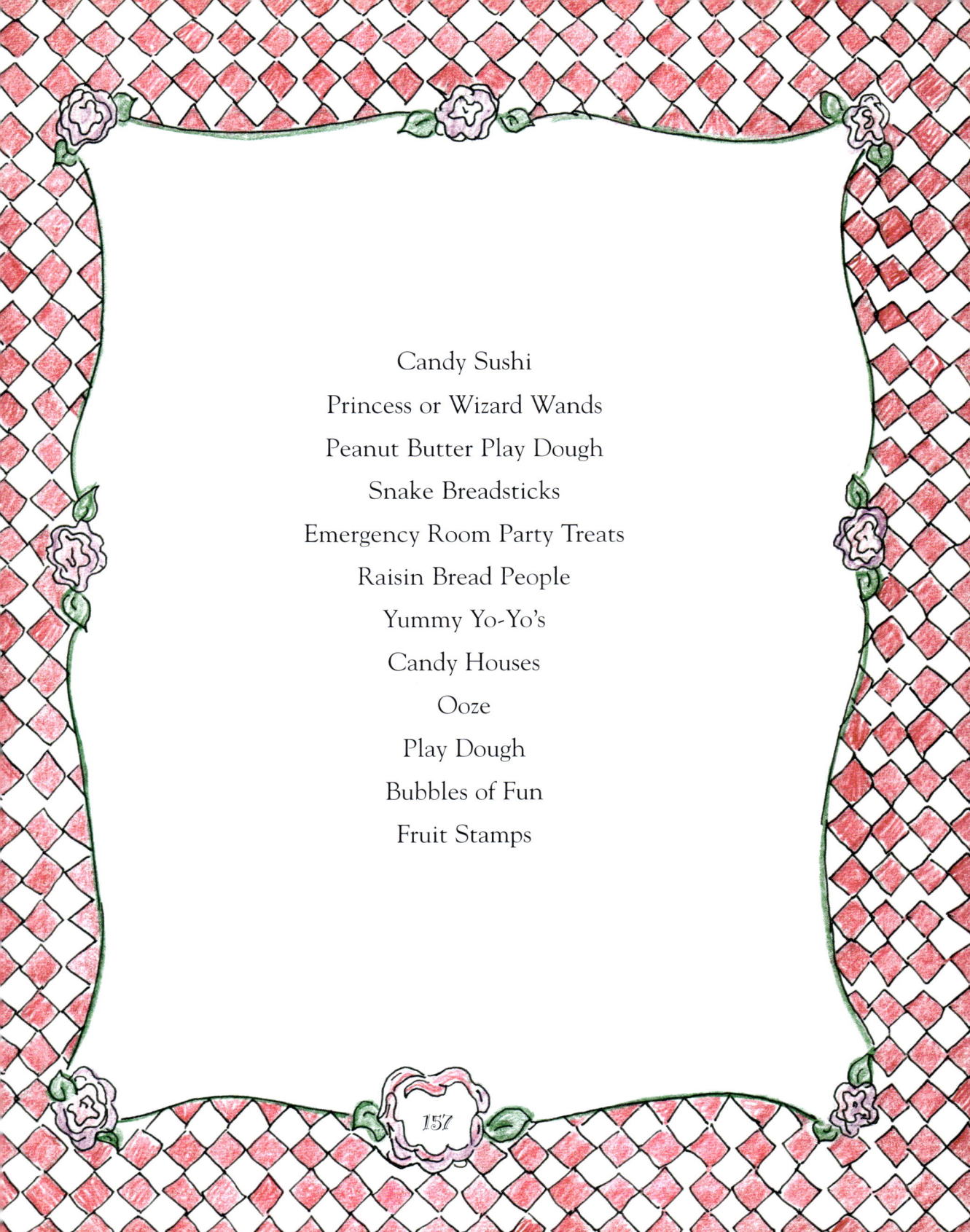

Candy Sushi

Princess or Wizard Wands

Peanut Butter Play Dough

Snake Breadsticks

Emergency Room Party Treats

Raisin Bread People

Yummy Yo-Yo's

Candy Houses

Ooze

Play Dough

Bubbles of Fun

Fruit Stamps

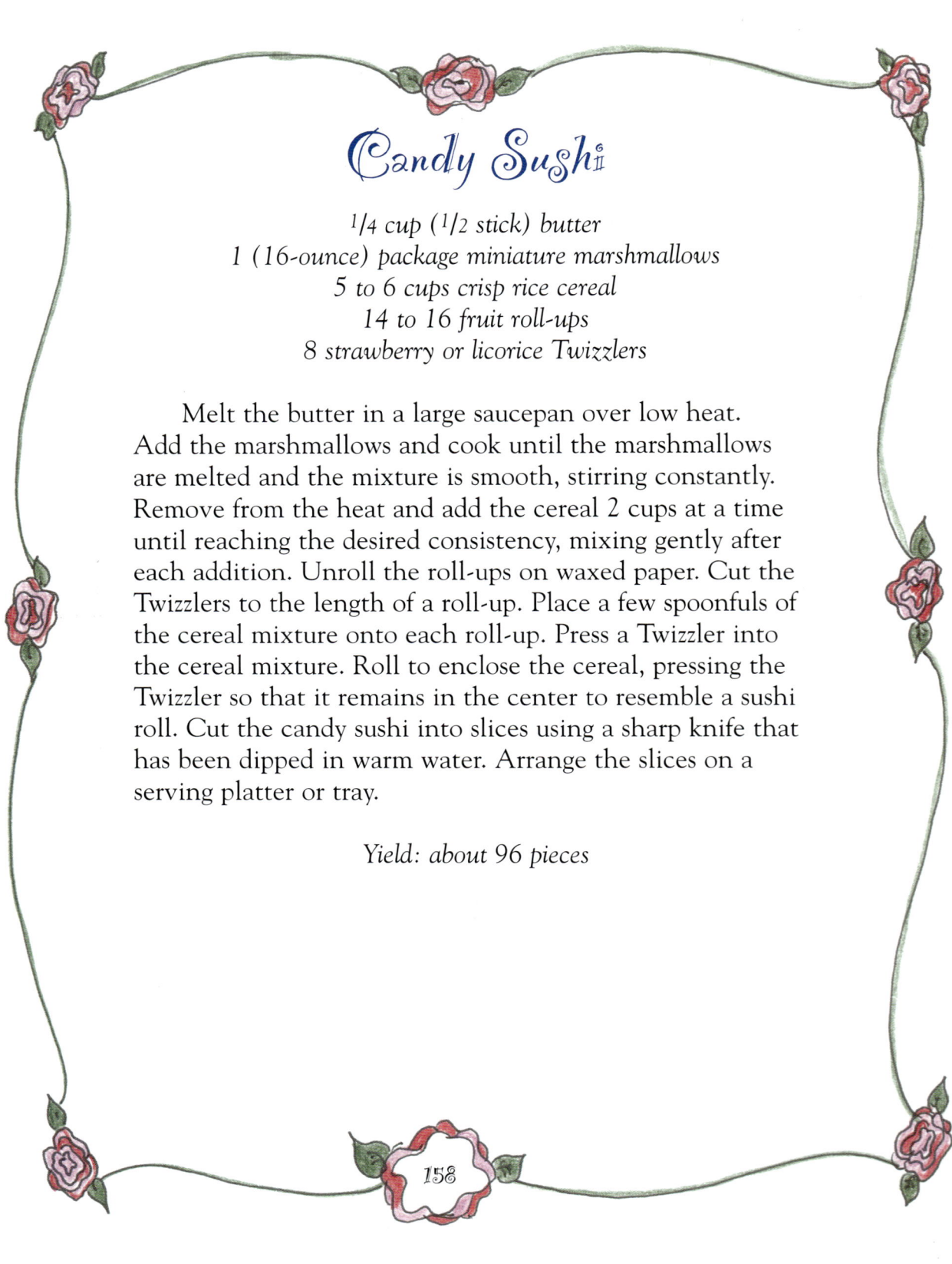

Candy Sushi

¹/4 cup (¹/2 stick) butter
1 (16-ounce) package miniature marshmallows
5 to 6 cups crisp rice cereal
14 to 16 fruit roll-ups
8 strawberry or licorice Twizzlers

Melt the butter in a large saucepan over low heat.
Add the marshmallows and cook until the marshmallows
are melted and the mixture is smooth, stirring constantly.
Remove from the heat and add the cereal 2 cups at a time
until reaching the desired consistency, mixing gently after
each addition. Unroll the roll-ups on waxed paper. Cut the
Twizzlers to the length of a roll-up. Place a few spoonfuls of
the cereal mixture onto each roll-up. Press a Twizzler into
the cereal mixture. Roll to enclose the cereal, pressing the
Twizzler so that it remains in the center to resemble a sushi
roll. Cut the candy sushi into slices using a sharp knife that
has been dipped in warm water. Arrange the slices on a
serving platter or tray.

Yield: about 96 pieces

Princess or Wizard Wands

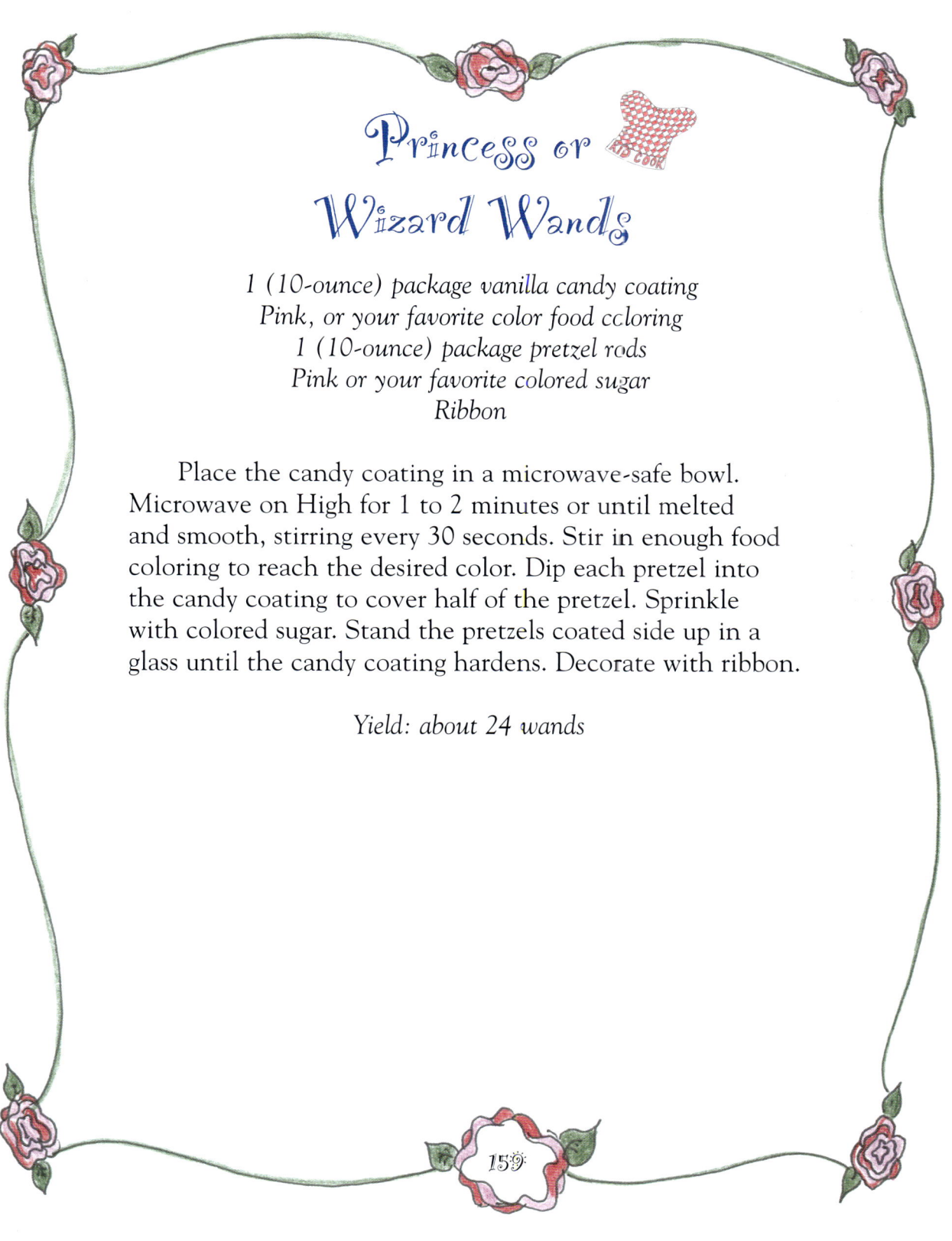

1 (10-ounce) package vanilla candy coating
Pink, or your favorite color food coloring
1 (10-ounce) package pretzel rods
Pink or your favorite colored sugar
Ribbon

Place the candy coating in a microwave-safe bowl. Microwave on High for 1 to 2 minutes or until melted and smooth, stirring every 30 seconds. Stir in enough food coloring to reach the desired color. Dip each pretzel into the candy coating to cover half of the pretzel. Sprinkle with colored sugar. Stand the pretzels coated side up in a glass until the candy coating hardens. Decorate with ribbon.

Yield: about 24 wands

Yawning

If you are yawning at the table, you should cover your mouth with your hand. Try getting into the conversation or drink some ice water to help wake you up.

Peanut Butter Play Dough

1 (4-ounce) package vanilla
instant pudding mix
1 cup milk
1/2 cup peanut butter
1 cup powdered milk

Combine the pudding mix and milk in a bowl and mix well. Add the peanut butter and powdered milk in the order listed, mixing well after each addition.

Yield: 2 1/2 cups

Snake  Breadsticks

1 loaf frozen bread dough, thawed
All-purpose flour
Raisins
1/3 cup margarine, melted
Red food coloring
Green food coloring

Divide the bread dough into six to eight equal portions. Dip each portion in the flour to coat. Roll each portion into a rope. Press two raisins into the end of each rope to form snake eyes. Combine half the margarine with red food coloring in a small bowl and mix well. Combine the remaining margarine with green food coloring in a small bowl and mix well. Decorate the dough ropes with the food coloring to resemble snakes. Arrange on a baking sheet. Bake at 350 degrees for 15 minutes.

Yield: 6 to 8 snakes

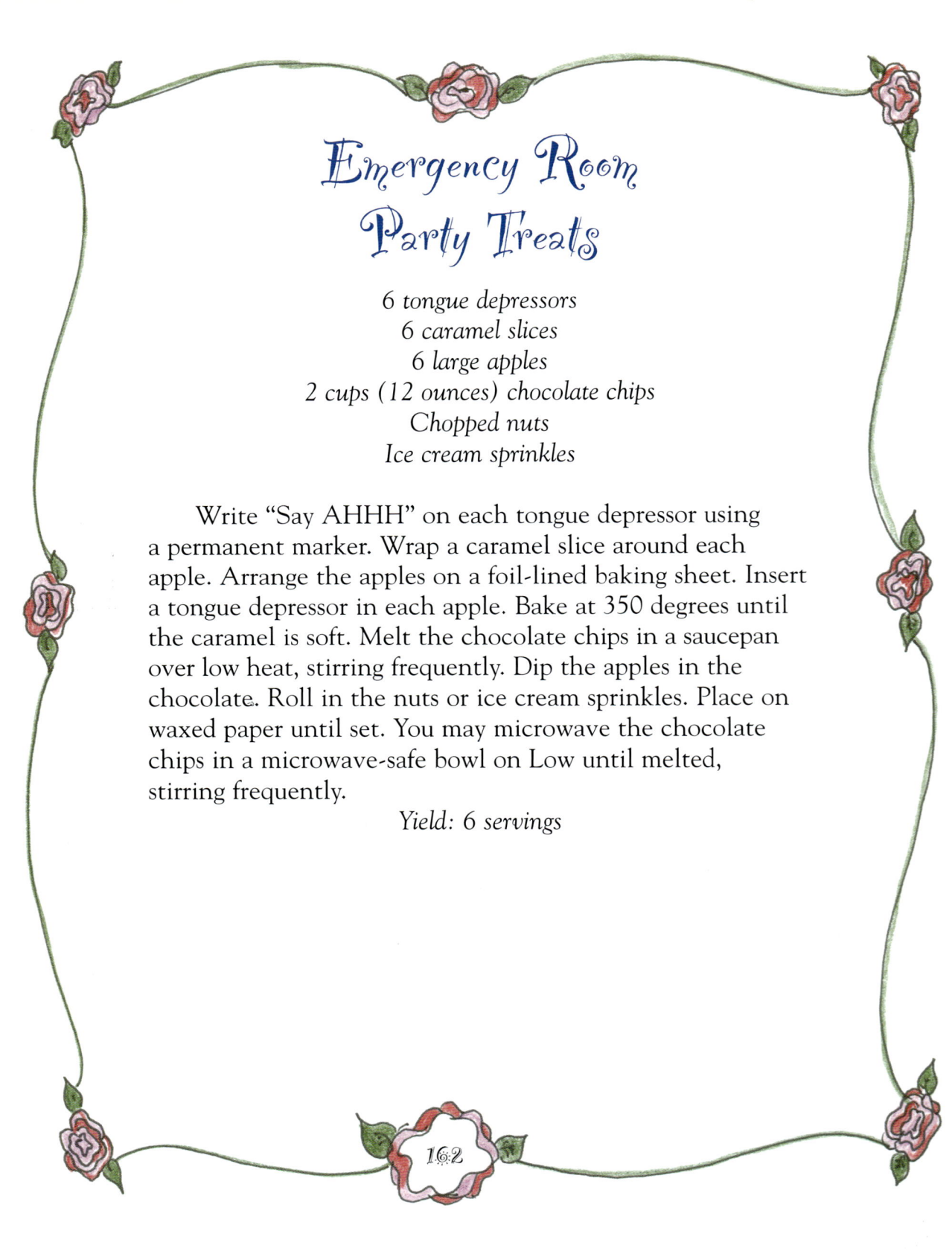

Emergency Room
Party Treats

6 tongue depressors
6 caramel slices
6 large apples
2 cups (12 ounces) chocolate chips
Chopped nuts
Ice cream sprinkles

Write "Say AHHH" on each tongue depressor using a permanent marker. Wrap a caramel slice around each apple. Arrange the apples on a foil-lined baking sheet. Insert a tongue depressor in each apple. Bake at 350 degrees until the caramel is soft. Melt the chocolate chips in a saucepan over low heat, stirring frequently. Dip the apples in the chocolate. Roll in the nuts or ice cream sprinkles. Place on waxed paper until set. You may microwave the chocolate chips in a microwave-safe bowl on Low until melted, stirring frequently.

Yield: 6 servings

Raisin Bread People

2 slices raisin bread
2 tablespoons cream cheese, softened
Raisins, nuts and maraschino cherries

Cut the bread into gingerbread-shaped men or women using a cookie cutter. Spread a thin layer of cream cheese over each shape. Decorate with raisins, nuts and cherries to make faces and buttons. You may substitute peanut butter for the cream cheese, if desired.

Yield: 2 raisin bread people

Yummy Yo-Yo's

3 tablespoons whipped cream cheese
1 teaspoon lemon juice
1/2 teaspoon sugar
10 gingersnaps
10 pieces red shoelace licorice

Combine the cream cheese, lemon juice and sugar in a bowl and beat until blended. Spread 2 teaspoons of the cream cheese mixture on one side of half the gingersnaps. Top with the remaining gingersnaps. Wind a licorice piece around the center of each to resemble a yo-yo string.

Yield: 5 yo-yos

Candy Houses

6 graham cracker squares
12 whole graham crackers
1 cup of your favorite frosting
Fruit Loops cereal
Assorted small candies, such as gumdrops or
"M & M's" Plain Chocolate Candies

Cut each graham cracker square into halves diagonally to form triangles. Lay two whole graham crackers side by side on a tray or work surface and "glue" together using the frosting. Arrange two graham cracker triangles at the top to form the roof, gluing with the frosting. Repeat the procedure with the remaining graham crackers. Decorate the houses with the cereal and candies using the frosting as glue.

Yield: 6 houses

$\star$oze

1/4 cup each white glue and warm water
4 or 5 drops of your favorite color food coloring
1 tablespoon borax powder
1/4 cup very warm water

Mix the glue, warm water and food coloring in a disposable cup. Mix the borax and very warm water in a disposable cup. Pour the borax mixture into the glue mixture and stir until the liquid is absorbed. Store in a sealable plastic bag. This recipe is not edible. Do not get it on carpet or clothing.

Yield: about 3/4 cup

Play Dough

2 cups each all-purpose flour and water
1 cup salt
1 teaspoon cream of tartar
2 tablespoons vegetable oil
1 teaspoon of your favorite color food coloring

Mix the ingredients in a saucepan. Cook over medium heat until the dough pulls from the side of the pan, stirring constantly. Remove from the heat and let cool. Knead for a few minutes on a work surface. Store, covered, in the refrigerator.

Yield: about 5 cups

Zzzzz

Snoozing at the table is inappropriate. If you are exhausted (really tired) and it is time to eat, it is probably in your best interest to ask to be excused from the meal and head on off to bed. And, of course, sweet dreams to you.

Bubbles of Fun

*5 cups water
1 cup scented liquid soap
1 cup light corn syrup
1 teaspoon glycerin*

Combine the water, liquid soap, corn syrup and glycerin in a large bowl and mix well.
Let stand for 8 to 10 hours for the best results.
Dip bubble blowers into the soap mixture and blow bubbles.

Yield: about 7 cups

Fruit Stamps

Firm fruit, such as apples or pears
Solid color fabric
Thick piece of felt or a blanket
Textile paint
Stiff paintbrush
Matchsticks

Slice the fruit in half and dry the cut surface with a towel. Place the fabric over the felt on a work surface. Brush the paint thickly on the cut side of the fruit. Press the painted side of the fruit onto the fabric. Paint the seeds of the fruit by dipping the end of a matchstick in a different color paint and pressing on the fabric.

Yield: a fun rainy day craft

Table of Measurements

= 3 teaspoons equal 1 tablespoon

= or 2 FL.OZS   4 tablespoons equal ¼ cup or 2 fluid ounces

= or ¼ LB   1 stick butter equals ½ cup or ¼ pound

= ½ PINT or 8 FL. OZS — 1 cup equals ½ pint or 8 fluid ounces

= 1 PINT or 16 FL OZS   2 cups equal 1 pint or 16 fluid ounces

= 1 QUART   4 cups equal 1 quart

= 1 POUND   4 cups flour equal 1 pound

= 1 POUND   2 cups sugar equal 1 pound

Formal

NAPKIN · SALAD FORK · DINNER FORK · BREAD AND BUTTER PLATE · BUTTER KNIFE · WINE GLASS · DINNER KNIFE · TEASPOON · SOUP SPOON · SEAFOOD FORK

Casual

BREAD & BUTTER · TUMBLER · NAPKIN · FORK · KNIFE · SPOON

Contributors

Kimberly Abeldt	Jennifer Blackmon	Suzanne Curtis
Annabel Adams	Amy Bone	Chalease Denson
Megan Adcock	Judie Bower	Kathryn Droder
Abbey Adkins	Ashley Bradley	Susan Dukes
Debbie Adkins	Cindy Brady	Brandon Durman
Emily Adkins	Kathy Bright	Dana Durman
Katie Adkinson	Marty Hagan Byrd	Patrick Durman
Jae Lyn Akin	Amy Carder	Holly Ethridge
Louree Alexander	Diane Carnes	Christy Evans
Charity Anglin	Claudia Carroll	April Feliciano
Kim Asad	Angie Coleman	Carissa Fisher
Jana Autry	Jim Connally	Heather Fletcher
Liz Ballard	Melisa Cooper	Lyndy Frost
Rebecca Ballard	Rachel Corley	Alexander Fry
Suzie Balser	Kim Costanza	Lynette Good
Cherie Barker	Stephanie Cotton	Terri Good
Kathy Bauman	Tammy Cowart	Ginger Haberle
Shelley Beaumont	Mary Ann Cozby	Amanda Habermehl
Sarah Beck	Meredith Cozby	Cassidy Hammer
Suzy Beck	Aaron Cullen	Madison Hammer
Shawn Bergfeld	Clayton Cullen	Vickie Hammer
Anne Bingham	Ronda Cullen	Kelly Haney
Amy Blackmon	Spencer Cullen	Marsha Harrison

Debbie Hartung

Emily Hegwood

Sandi Hegwood

Amy Hendricks

Susan Hene

Diane Hodge

Kim Holley

Carrie Hunt

Ransom Jarvis

Cadie Johnson

Kenya Johnson

Beth Jouett

Tana Kay

Zoe Kerr

P. J. Lamb

Crysti LaRocca

Elizabeth Lisso

Debbie Matteucci

Junella McClusky

Luci Mimms

Amber Moden

Kate Newberry

Jennifer Noble

Deanna Olson

Sarah Jones Olvey

Paige Parrish

Monica Penkilo

Rachel Plotkin

Katie Powell

Sara Powell

Lisa Preddy

Brittani Pruitt

Jeanne Ramunni

Nicole Richards

Krista Richardson

Jennifer Rippy

Haleigh Roberts

Madeline Roberts

Mary Leigh Roberts

Mary Margaret Roberts

Meredith Roberts

Lou Ann Rockwell-Huseth

Sandra Rojas

Jeny Romines

Teri Sawyer

Kristen Seeber

Julie Shamburger

Emma Short

Hampton Short

Holly Short

Lynne Short

Deanna Simms

Tonya Skrocki

Jenny Sloan

Gayle Steiner

Leann Strnadel

Janet Taylor

Joan Hertz Taylor

Marketta Tefteller

Andra Willmon Terburgh

The Discovery Science Place

Allison Andrews Thompson

Julie Thompson

Jennifer Walsh

Greta Watkins

Jennifer Watkins

Leslie Watson

Shurrell Wiebe

Vickie Williams

Index

174

Ring Around the Rosie

JUNIOR LEAGUE OF TYLER, INC.

1919 South Donnybrook
Tyler, Texas 75701
Telephone: 903-593-8141
Fax: 903-595-1362

Name _____

Street Address _____

City _____ State _____ Zip _____

Telephone _____

YOUR ORDER	QTY	TOTAL
Ring Around the Rosie at $21.95 per book		$
Shipping & handling at $5.00 for first book; $1.00 for each additional book		$
	TOTAL	$

Method of Payment: [   ] MasterCard   [   ] VISA

[   ] Check enclosed payable to Junior League of Tyler, Inc.

Account Number _____ Expiration Date _____

Signature _____

Photocopies accepted.

176